I0627114

A
HUNTER'S DREAM

A HUNTER'S DREAM

A TRUJILLO

Parlyaree Press
Atlanta, Georgia
www.parlyaree.com

Library of Congress Cataloging-in-Publication Data
Names: Trujillo, A .
Title: A HUNTER'S DREAM / A Trujillo
Description: First Edition | Atlanta : Parlyaree Press, 2025
Identifiers: LCCN: applied for | ISBN 9781961206236 (paperback)
Subjects: LCGFT: Novels
LC record available at https://lccn.loc.gov/

Design by Parlyaree Press
Some imagery liscensed from Adobe Stock.

Front Cover/Title Typeface is HWT Antique Tuscan 9.
Interior Text Typeface is Adobe Garamond.

Paperback ISBN: 978-1-961206-23-6
Ebook ISBN: 987-1-961206-24-3

To Sandy.

A
HUNTER'S DREAM
A TRUJILLO

Bastián nudged a deeply tanned finger at the ceramic cup of sake. He wasn't in a drinking mood. They had been at sea for almost a year. Even after a month on land, the last thing he wanted to do was remind himself of the headache and nausea.

He glanced to the rest of his team: the inept crew the hunter's guild had assigned him to lead. They all drank and cheered, celebrating their latest job well-done. But it had been nothing. Expelling an akaname from a home that the owner should have simply cleaned. Hardly worth their time. They had been sent here on a mission. *He* had been sent on a mission. These jobs were just filler for the large game they were to hunt.

One of his team members noticed his demure state and broke off from the group. A tall muscular man with an imposing stature sat down next to him. Bastián would have thought the brute attractive if his voice didn't grate against his ears every time he spoke.

"Is an Asturias too important to share a drink with his subordinates?" Frederick jabbed.

"We've done nothing worth celebrating," Bastián said curtly. He was always short with Frederick, the one his father had told him to be particularly watchful of. His peer wanted to make his own name known, no matter the cost.

"We made it across the largest ocean. That's for hell sure something."

"Not without casualties," Bastián said.

"Yeah, well, they weren't the best of us, anyway," Frederick said. "Plus, you can't argue that seven members isn't easier to handle than ten."

Bastián scowled, disgusted at Frederick's disregard for their lost crew members. Bastián didn't have too much care for them, either, but he certainly wouldn't voice that.

"I don't make a habit out of celebrating deaths," Bastián said. "We landed a month ago and we've not made any progress."

"Progress?" Frederick laughed. "We've been welcomed into a foreign land and given steady work. What is there to complain about?"

Bastián closed his eyes, one blue and one an odd yellowish green. "That's not what we came here to do."

"That's not what you came here to do," Frederick corrected, taking his untouched sake. He drank it in a crude gulp with liquid running from the corner of his mouth and into his beard.

"My father gave explicit instructions for us to investigate the rumor an oni has infiltrated the royal family of Yasunai."

"But who said you had to do that? Who is checking in on you? We were both on that ship. No one is making that journey just to see if we follow through."

"Maybe not you, but—"

Frederick laughed. "What? For you?" He laughed again. "I know your daddy caught you with the Morales boy. I know that's really why he sent you across the ocean with a vague lead. And the rest of us? We all wanted to get away for our own reasons. Or had to. So, no. No one's checking on us, including you, last son of House Asturias."

Bastián took the sake cup back from him, refilled it, and drank. That wasn't the reason. His father wouldn't care about that. If his father were that critical, there were plenty other things to judge him on. He clutched a locket around his neck as if funneling his anger into it.

"You all seek redemption," Bastián said. "And I'm here to make sure you get it."

Frederick was unbothered. "Redemption? Ha. Thieves, disgraces to their families, and maybe an 'accidental' injury to another hunter—" Frederick spoke the last especially flippantly. "—nothing that serious. If it was, don't think they'd send you to supervise. Face it. You're just like us. Wear those fancy clothes all you want but I know the Asturias name holds little significance anymore."

"My father—"

"Is a joke," Frederick finished for him. "And a boring lecturer. You may still have some secrets, but I know he wasn't pulled off hunts by choice. That tells me the guild wants to keep an eye on him."

Bastián clutched his hand into a fist. He had always known his father, Vincente Asturias, as a scholar and teacher rather than practicing the cruel and ruthless extermination tactics that had helped his grandfather establish the hunter's guild. Those like Frederick flirted dangerously close to the truth of why and Bastián had no intention of letting them get closer to it.

Bastián hadn't noticed how hard he had been gripping the ceramic cup until he heard it crack under his hand. Damn it. Usually, right after a full moon was the time he felt most relaxed and focused. Must be having a leftover twinge of heightened irritation.

"It doesn't matter what you think of me or my family," Bastián said. "As the leader—"

"Right. The 'leader,'" Frederick griped. "*I* was supposed to be made captain. I was before you jumped on board last minute and took charge."

"You pointed that out to me enough on the ship. How many times was it? Once, twice, a day?"

Frederick's casual demeanor faltered but he kept up his taunt. "I'm glad not to be in charge. A great fortune, actually. Don't have to be the one making decisions and taking blame."

Bastián eyed him severely. Frederick would never readily admit blame for anything. Bastián believed that had to be why the change in leadership was made.

"Our duty is to our guild," Bastián said evenly. "We begin the search tomorrow."

Frederick lifted his hands in faux defeat, and Bastián observed smug amusement on his face. Bastián's father didn't send him away. Full stop. Vincente had the tendency to be stern and severe when dealing with monsters and guild members, but he had always loved his son.

Bastián ran his thumb along a ring on his index finger, a habit when calming his nerves. No. His father was very loyal to him. And yet why had he seemingly tossed him out into the ocean? Bastián's anger was mostly fueled by the fact he didn't know the answer either. For his father and the guild, he'd hunt down this cunning monster and prove himself worthy of returning to his homeland a victor.

Bastián fiddled with his locket as he waited for his crew to arrive the next day, snapping it open and then closed. He regarded the metal pendant with both reverence and disdain, unlike the ring for which he only felt gratitude. He had brought extra wolfsbane and soothing oil, though he hadn't needed them since they landed. Lucky, as he had used half the supply on the trip over here. He had felt like a feline woefully afraid of water and had needed the extra help in keeping calm. He held no affection for the sea and doubted he'd be anything but a land-dwelling creature.

Once his crew arrived, Bastián brought them to the nearest temple. This was a practice which he happily observed taught by his father: respect the land's spirits and abide by their rules. What would a yokai care about a crucifix or holy water? The guild's elders staunchly disagreed and expected any creature to bow to their sacraments.

Bastián walked the steps to the shrine and realized he heard no footsteps behind him. He turned around to see his crew stopped and murmuring amongst themselves.

"Is there a reason you're all huddled there?" Bastián asked.

No one said anything. A few avoided eye contact as if a child afraid the teacher would call on them to answer. Frederick's face held the opposite as he struck an authoritative stance, his burly frame blocking the steps so none could come up to Bastián's side.

"This is asinine," Frederick said. "You disrespect the guild by praying to other gods."

He gave him a stern look. "We must honor a country's traditions before we embark. Spirits often follow them, too. A small nuance in the local beliefs could be the downfall of a powerful demon. It is best to have their blessing."

Frederick crossed his arms. "You act as if we're here to appease monsters rather than hunt them. No wonder your father is a disgrace to the guild. Can't say I'm surprised that his son is the same."

"Then stay here," Bastián said, suppressing a primal growl. "I won't be long."

Bastián tried to block out his crew's gossipy whispers as he continued to the shrine. He knelt at the altar and took deep, calming breaths. Soon he slipped into a peaceful state. His focus was solely on himself and the altar before him. From his pack, he took a small bouquet of irises and daffodils wrapped delicately in paper. He placed a couple ume and a mandarin next to the flowers. The orange of the fruits complemented the bright blue and yellow petals.

He whispered a quick prayer—simple and nondescript. He did not truly know the gods of this place, and he knew spirits did not appreciate any pretense. Bastián rose from the altar and proceeded down the steps of the temple.

Before he reached his waiting crew, a voice called for him to stop. Bastián saw a short, balding man who held a soft and kind look on his face.

"Young hunter," the monk said, "may I speak with you a moment?"

Not wanting to hear another remark from Frederick, Bastián held his palm up. Even if he couldn't see it, he was certain he could feel Frederick's glare on his back.

"Walk with me," the monk said, catching Bastián's attention again and leading him through the temple's garden.

Bastián followed, silently waiting for the monk's next question. They walked through the temple grounds without speaking. The monk paused several times to gaze over a pond or whisper a thankful blessing to a cricket. Bastián followed wherever his gaze landed during these moments and tried to focus on the tranquility.

"What blessing did you seek?" asked the monk.

"The standard I do in all regions with which I am unfamiliar. First an apology for my ignorance. Then an ask for greater understanding. Next a benediction for safe passage. And finally, a gratitude for listening and opening any doors, natural or unnatural."

"You do not ask them for help with your quarry?"

"When your job is to expel, exorcise, or exterminate spirits," Bastián said, "I think it would be a show of bad manners to ask spirits to aid in it. If they wish to offer any aid, they may."

"You are humble, beast of the West. The world needs more hunters like you. Ones who seek to understand first instead of destroy."

Beast. "You know who I am?"

"But, of course," he said with a chuckle. "It was our monastery who approved your father's request. We have had a few Western hunters, so we know your dress style. And you dress with markedly more prestige than the others."

Bastián looked down at his clothes. He had never noticed the differences before. He always assumed them to be subtle. But now he studied his clothing: buckles and straps of the highest materials that remained intact unlike those of his crew, his vest and pants weather-resistant—though he had put that through a test many times and they seldom passed—boots well-broken in but fit to his feet and calves perfectly. Leathers were well-oiled so they kept a sheen to them, long brown coat of the sturdiest material, and even his hat ended in an embellishment no one else had.

He had conflicted feelings growing up as an Asturias. How it caused his peers to think him arrogant or ill-tempered. Or worse, assume he was equal to his father and challenge him despite being only several years past his twentieth birthday. He always won, but that wasn't the point. He hadn't realized just how much he carried that wealth with him.

"You are travelling to Yasunai, correct?" the monk said with concern in his voice.

"Yes," Bastián confirmed. "Why do you sound so grave?"

"Yasunai is not kind to outsiders. Even those within our country. I fear neither the gods nor your talismans can grant your safety there."

Bastián doubted the monk but did not want to be disrespectful. Even the weakest of his crew knew how to channel basic magic through their talismans. At least enough for an extra layer of self-defense against foes, be them monster or human.

"There is a rumor my father told me about," Bastián said. "It originates there."

"I know the one of which you speak. It is the only one that would interest a hunter as famous as Asturias and yet be as unsubstantiated to not come himself."

"Do you believe it's true? Is there a demon in the royal family of Yukimura?"

"It does not matter," the monk said, shaking his head. "You must go there regardless."

"Why do you say that?"

He lifted his finger in front of Bastián as if to touch something.

"The other end of your thread is there," he said, dropping his finger.

"My thread?"

Bastián looked to where the monk had pointed but saw nothing.

"Yes." The monk stood from the bench and ushered Bastián along. "We have spoken enough. You should return to your companions."

"No, wait," Bastián said. "I don't know what you're talking about."

The monk continued walking back to the front of the temple, sure the hunter would follow. "Trust that the spirits of this land have indeed heard your prayers. They will help as long as your intentions remain pure."

Bastián quickly followed, surprised at how fast the small man could walk while appearing effortless. *Remain pure?* Was hunting pure? Bastián doubted that. Noble, maybe, but could anything that involved violence be thought of as having pure intentions? He thought about questioning more, but they were already back at the temple entrance and his scattered crew were whispering amongst themselves like co-conspirators.

The monk stopped him with an outstretched hand. Bastián nearly fell over.

"Hunter," he said, "bear this in mind: If you are ever in

desperation, follow the red thread. I wish you luck on this journey you've been bound to."

Bastián nodded and, not knowing what else to do, gave a bow. His crew had shut up and now eyed him with…disdain? Maybe he was being too suspicious of them, but they surely didn't like him getting special treatment. Frederick still stood blocking the path. He didn't move when Bastián approached. The two locked eyes, and, after a few moments of this posturing, Frederick stepped aside, arms still crossed and let Bastián lead them on.

CHAPTER 2

With the monk's warning echoing in his mind, Bastián led his crew onward to Yasunai. The longer they travelled together, the more Bastián thought the warning felt like a self-fulfilling prophecy. He only trusted two of the hunters to be effective scouts, the other three to maintain their cart and supplies. That left him and Frederick. Despite Bastián's desire to keep far away from the recalcitrant hunter, he knew him to be the most skilled to fight off any attack—aside from Bastián himself.

Bastián meticulously detailed their journey each night. He noted any celestial markers, keeping track of the lunar phases. It was a habit he had formed as an adolescent. One, he thought, would keep him alive. *Waxing gibbous with only a small sliver darkened out, a good time for a new journey with a clear mind.*

He used the notebook as his personal bestiary, too. He sketched out every encounter he had with a preternatural being. For this trip though, he was light on additions to it, having encountered more human-made traps than ghastly creatures since entering Yasunai. He had documented a few of these, but he quickly lost interest in the amateur assembly each trap had.

When they camped, Bastián sat separately from the rest. He updated his journal even if the only entry was the distance traveled that day. He heard laughter from where his crew were gathered around a sphere of light hovering six inches off the ground. They were smart not to light any fires—Bastián's orders—so they made do with the ball Frederick produced. Only he and Bastián were skilled enough in the magical arts to use spellcasting for a practical purpose. Bastián let the novice hunters be in awe of Frederick's abilities. He felt no need to show off to them.

Bastián idly sketched a cat-like creature in the journal. He did this as if he were bored during a lecture and doodling in the margins of his notes. He had often done that during his schooling, even when his father led the class. He had already learned much more from his father than the generalized lessons allowed.

The heavy crunch of dry leaves interrupted Bastián's meditative sketching and he looked up to see Frederick walking towards him with a slight stagger to his gait. Of course, they had been drinking while on a hunt. Bastián didn't try to hide the scowl that reflexively affected his face. He'd have to find out which of these amateurs Frederick convinced to omit alcohol from the inventory list. Instead of stopping in front of him, Frederick took one step past him. Bastián heard faint rustling of clothing before the distinctive sound and thick smell of urine made him jump from his spot.

"You should join us," Frederick said before Bastián could leave.

"You shouldn't be drinking on a hunt."

"What hunt?" said Frederick. "We haven't gotten to kill anything since we left. This isn't a hunt yet. It's a leisurely stroll. And *someone's* gotta keep morale up."

Bastián pressed his hand against his forehead, feeling a headache coming on from dealing with Frederick's insolence. Gratefully he heard the stream go weak and stop, but the smell still hung in the air.

"Speaking of morale, I've been telling stories about you," Frederick continued, turning around as he finished fixing his clothing. "They're really enjoying it."

"What stories could you possibly have to tell about me?"

"Only have a few," Frederick admitted, "but they particularly enjoyed the one about how you like to take it up the ass with other men."

Bastián's face turned red out of anger not embarrassment. "You have no idea what I do in my private life."

"Don't take it so hard. Makes them fear you less." Frederick laughed. "But I suppose taking it hard is your thing."

"Do you regret not outing me to our superiors or something?" Bastián snapped.

"Of course, not," Frederick said. "Just think people should be honest about who they are. Especially if they're asked to lead."

Frederick gripped his shoulder in a condescending pat that turned quickly into him wiping his hand on Bastián's leather outer coat. A disgusted shudder ran down his spine. He felt an immediate need to clean and oil the leather, a ritual he usually reserved for after a successful hunt. With such an incompetent crew, he was beginning to doubt this hunt would be one of those successes.

Three days into their journey, one of those flimsy traps caught something. Not a monster, but a Yasunai guard scout. A novice of their crew alerted him, and Bastián attempted to calm the angry man. He could see Frederick in his periphery, as if circling them like a vulture. He loosened the scout's bindings, but kept his hands and feet tied out of caution.

"How did you get caught in your own trap?" Bastián had to ask.

Frederick quickly appeared by his side just as the scout began to speak. "Oh, that wasn't one of theirs. I had Josephine set it up."

"Neither of you told me you were laying traps."

"Not worth getting your ego bruised," Frederick said. "Just a common trap, for predator or prey. Food or, well, this."

Bastián looked at Frederick's broad smile with skepticism. He was enjoying this a suspicious amount.

"We're not going to hurt you," Bastián assured their captive. "We're here to help, in truth. Will you take a message to your emperor for us?"

"You'll let me go if I do that?"

Bastián nodded. "We're hunters. Capable ones, as you can see. However, you can no doubt get to your emperor quicker on your own than we can without knowing this land. Bring a message explaining our reason for being here. That's all we ask."

"Yes, I will do that."

"Good decision."

Bastián walked to the supply cart and took out writing equipment. He began drafting a message. He needed to take his time and choose his wording carefully. He remembered the warnings about this area. If the emperor were to comply with their mission, he needed to appeal to both ego and pragmatism. Bastián read over the draft, congratulating himself on the prose. He always thought he could be eloquent when writing.

Shouting. He dropped the letter. Shouting and…gagging? He rushed back to his crew.

"Stop!" Bastián yelled at the sight before him. "What the hell are you doing?!"

But Bastián was too late. Frederick stood with his whip tightened around the scout's throat. The poor man's neck had turned purple, and his eyes bulged from their sockets. Frederick released the pressure from the whip and the scout fell limply to the ground.

"You trust too easily," Frederick explained matter-of-factly. "He was likely going to rat us out to the nearest guard post. Better him than us."

"You didn't have to do that!" Bastián insisted. "He was going to send a message!"

"Well, now we just sent one," Frederick said with a kick to the corpse.

Bastián knelt by the body, panic building in his gut. He didn't know what to do. In frantic whispers, he begged the spirits for forgiveness. He hadn't known this man. Maybe he had been a violent one himself. But life was taken without cause. He had posed no threat.

He closed the body's eyes and maneuvered the corpse onto its back. He couldn't perform a full burial, but he began placing rocks over the body. Though maybe he should grab some shrubbery, too. Both a respectful and hidden funeral.

A whistle, like one calling a dog, stopped him, and Bastián looked over his shoulder. His crew had gone, taking the cart with them. They had left him. But he was their leader. He hastily followed and, when he caught up, could see Frederick at the helm. At least the arrogant man didn't bother turning around to give Bastián a cocky smile.

Bastián could feel his authority over the crew slipping. After that night, the older two stuck to Frederick's side, showering him with undue praise. Only the three novices were hesitant to defy Bastián, but he could tell the more gullible of them were being drawn to Frederick more each day. Frederick knew this, too, and he never hesitated to flash him a smug grin or taunting wink. Though Bastián preferred that over the predatory glower his peer gave him when he thought Bastián couldn't see it.

One night, as Bastián sat apart from the others, he swore he saw something moving amongst the trees. He stood to get a better view. His ears picked up a whistling sound, and he dodged out of the way just in time to avoid a star-shaped blade that splintered the tree behind him.

He yelled it was an ambush, but the warning wasn't heard over the cries of his crew. He cast a protection spell, and another blade bounced off his magic shield. When it was safe, he went to his crew to find most of them cowering, never having faced real combat before. Frederick was an exception as he carelessly shot spell after spell with a manic look in his eyes.

Bastián grabbed his arm and cast a blinding light, giving them a brief moment to recompose.

"Focus!" he shouted to his companion.

Frederick looked surprised, then he scowled and shoved Bastián to the ground. He hit hard, and his breath rushed from him. Frederick raised a hand covered in magical energy. Bastián could barely move his neck to see it, but it looked like it was pointed at him.

Before Bastián could find out, a weighted rope shot from the tree cover and wrapped around Frederick's arm. He cried out, more in surprise than pain, as the magic smoldered and died out. Suppression wards. Their attackers knew they had magic and knew how to stop them from using it.

Bastián recovered but was met with a spear inches from his face. He instinctively tried to back away, but his arms were painfully grabbed and tied behind him. The coarse rope harshly bit into his skin as it was pulled tight. His eyes searched for his crew and found them all in a similar state. Guardsmen were either pinning them down, securing them with rope, or both. Desperation hit him as he was dragged to his feet. This was the end. He had failed before even reaching the palace.

After the remaining hunters were secured, they were forced to stand in their binds and walk, surrounded by the soldiers. They received a crack of a whip or hit of the end of a spear if they protested or fell behind. Bastián kept up and said nothing. He knew this proceeding. He had been warned about the militaristic ways of

Yasunai, but he had let the quiet of the first few nights lull him into a false sense of safety. A small part of him still believed if he stated his purpose, the guard would let him speak to the emperor and let them carry out the investigation.

They walked a short distance, stopping before a line of mounted guards. The horses all pawed at the ground or shifted restlessly. Only one, separated from the others, lazily stood still. On top of those mounts, the guardsmen wore heavier armor than their foot soldier counterparts. All except the one mounted on the calm horse whose armor was light and the robe a brilliant purple rather than the common blue. Bastián could tell he was remarkably lean even under the metal plating. The soldiers shoved the captive hunters into their own line in front of them. They then forced them on their knees, kicking the back of the legs of the unlucky ones at the start of the line.

Bastián tried to produce a flame. He had to try. No luck. His magic was bound, too. The soldiers may not be able to summon magic of their own, but they knew to be cautious enough to imbue their ropes with wards. He was in a foreign land unable to reach his weapons, unable to access his magic, with imperial soldiers waiting to decide his fate. He was powerless. He had become powerless so quickly.

"Now, now," a melodic voice said, "you don't need to be so harsh. We shouldn't damage the stock too much."

A voice more theatrical than the short commands of the guards, Bastián held no surprise it came from the one in purple. Despite a clear want to appear distinguished, his black hair was tied back in a long ponytail with wisps that messily strayed from it and framed his gaunt face. The young man dismounted, helped by a guard, and approached the line. Bastián held back a sneer.

Royalty, no doubt, Bastián thought. *Can't even dismount a horse by himself.*

The noble's oddly red-brown eyes swept across the hunters like a curator who could never find anything good enough to put in his museum. There was something in his eyes that surprised Bastián, a look of profound tiredness maybe, but he only caught a glimpse, staring back down at the ground as soon as the man looked his direction. Bastián continued to covertly study the man whenever he turned his gaze from Bastián's spot in the lineup.

"This little troupe of yours," the nobleman said, "hunters, yes?"

No answer.

"Oh, someone has to be willing to confirm it."

"Yes," Josephine said weakly.

"And where might you be from?"

"Shinkawa."

He waved his hand, and she was hit.

A flinch from the nobleman? After his own order? Bastián certainly couldn't have seen that correctly.

"No. Where are you *actually* from? Clearly not anywhere on this island."

With no response, the soldier prepared to hit her again.

"Across the ocean," Bastián said. "We sailed from Oculito."

"Hm," he mused. "That is a long way. My father's buyers will be pleased. It's rare to find your stock around here."

The young man walked the line, eying each person. He paused at Frederick, noticing the whip at his side.

"Oh, what's this?" he said. "You were the ones to kill our scout, weren't you?"

He stood over Frederick, waiting for an answer. The hunter shot him an evil glare.

"Ask him," Frederick said with a violent tilt of his head toward Bastián. "He's our leader. We have nothing to do with his decisions."

The noble looked in the direction he pointed. He noticed the fine wears on Bastián and went to him. He knelt in front of him to get a better look.

He thumbed the collar of his jacket and lightly flicked the metal at his chest. "Clothing of fine material. And a hunter who seems to know what a tailor is. Not often you find that combination. A family crest, too." He trailed a cold finger under his chin and lifted his head up so their eyes met. "You were someone important, weren't you?"

"We were sent to—" Bastián tried to explain.

A soldier hit the back of his head. "His highness didn't ask."

Bastián briefly saw a frown on his face. He was certain of it. The young man tilted Bastián's head back up to look into his pained eyes. The noble's hand felt like ice, and his thin fingers made it feel like a skeleton was touching him. *Honestly,* Bastián thought, *with the way his cheeks and eyes sunk into his gaunt face, that description wasn't far from the truth.*

"It doesn't matter anymore," Bastián said without inflection. "Whomever I was is not who I am now."

"Oh? I suppose that's true." He moved Bastián's head from side to side, examining his heterochromia. "Eyes of two colors. A rare one, I see. You'd surely cause a tense auction. A shame I won't see how much you go for." He stood up slowly, bracing as he did, like a man decades older than he appeared. His amusement seemed to have dwindled, but his voice remained strangely airy, albeit notably more forced than it had been before. "Boys, wrap this one up for me."

"Sir," one guard said, "I'd advise—"

The young man raised his hand, silencing him. "I made my decision. I'll take that one myself."

The light-framed man turned from the group then gave a flourish as he twirled back around to the line, as if this were a stage performance. He clapped his hands with a smile that didn't quite reach his eyes.

"Okay, this is how it will go. Some of you will survive to be sold off as slaves. Some of you will…. Well, you'll be less alive. My apologies, but it turns out you can put a price on human life, and not everyone sells for high enough to make it worth the effort. But, for those, just think: at least you won't be a slave."

Bastián clenched his eyes shut. He should say something. Protest this. Do something as their leader. He heard cries of fear and disbelief from his crew. He also heard the punishment for it.

Was he truly a coward? Was he the poor leader Frederick had assumed he would be? He tried to will himself to act, but his fight was depleted.

Slowly, the noble made his way down the line. He scanned each hunter with a fabricated cheerfulness on his words. Created out of command or personal distaste, Bastián was uncertain but the more he heard it, the more it sounded fake.

"Mm. Nice bone structure and well-muscled. Market will love you…. What a rich skin tone on this one. They'll buy you just for that. Market…. Oh honey, you're just too adorable. All bright-eyed and eager. Kill…. Yup. Someone will enjoy you. Market…. Ugh, no, disgusting. Please kill it…. And you, there's just something about your face I don't like. Kill."

As the young noble finished his assessment, he ordered the soldiers to take each group to their new—or final—destinations. He stood by his horse and a guard promptly knelt to help him onto it. Bastián couldn't even grimace with disgust before a particularly gruff guard grabbed his arm and yanked him upright.

He watched his former crew depart. None turned to look back at him. He couldn't blame them. He had been their leader, and he had failed them. The guard pushed him toward the confiscated cart, and Bastián followed behind at a slow trod.

CHAPTER 3

Bastián had lived without financial worry, but this was his first time seeing a palace. Cherry trees and maples dotted the courtyard. Black sloping triangular roofs were stacked atop each other, contrasting with the white of the outer walls. Bastián was used to seeing the stone castles that were depicted in his reference books. He thought of them as dreary places concerned more with keeping others out rather than celebrating the life within. He'd call the vibrancy of the palace welcoming had he not been dragged here against his will.

Bastián was pulled abruptly left, forced away from the long line of stairs leading toward the central entrance. He was ushered through a small archway at the side of the palace.

He was brought to a bathhouse and told to strip. He refused. The guards repeated their order. He refused again, clutching his arms to his sides. One hit him with an open palm and grabbed at his coat. He tried his best to be firm and calm. He couldn't back down from this. He really couldn't.

With his focus on the guard, he didn't notice another man enter. An older man, dressed unlike a soldier. His long garments swept the floor with a whisper at each step as he approached the altercation.

"Leave," the dignified man said.

The guards didn't move.

"His highness requested his new servant remain unharmed."

"He's a hunter," one of them spat. "If he doesn't forfeit his belongings, he's dangerous to his *highness*. Let us do our jobs."

The older man looked toward the frightened hunter. "If we allow him some dignity, he will offer up his possessions. Surely he is smart enough to understand his situation."

Bastián's eyes shifted between the old man and the guards. The older man may not be nobility himself, but given that he could influence the guardsmen, Bastián knew it would benefit him to accept his offer. He nodded.

"Excellent." The man turned to the guards. "Please excuse us. I will ensure he will not pose a threat."

The main guard grumbled. He turned on his feet to leave but swiftly turned back and grabbed the magic talisman that was pinned to Bastián's chest, tearing it off. He held it up proudly.

"Now you can take over."

With an arrogant sneer, he led the other guards out of the bathhouse. Once they were gone, the older man addressed Bastián.

"My name is Aito, guardian of prince Eisuke, third son of our imperial majesty. You may think your capture unfortunate, but consider it lucky our master has favored you. Indeed, that luck can grow depending on how you behave. Eisuke demands little from his servants, especially his favorite ones. You will have an easy life here."

Bastián bit his tongue. He didn't want to be anyone's favored servant. They had already stripped him of his weapons. Now they took his magic. He thought he could physically overwhelm this older man, albeit he did look spry for his age. Likely a former soldier. And if he did, what then? He decided against making a rash decision and nodded to signify his understanding.

"Good. Now, I do have to ask that you undress and bathe. I will provide you with new clothing."

"Is there any chance I could ask you to face away as I do so?"

Aito shook his head. "I am not foolish enough to turn my back to a hunter."

Bastián slowly started to disrobe, grimacing as he did so. He paused, gripping his necklace. He hadn't been without it for over a decade. Favored servant? He doubted he would become complacent, but in the slim chance he did, he needed this deadline. He placed the necklace on top of the growing pile of clothing.

This rumination almost made him undo his pants without a second thought. Almost. He took a deep breath. It might be over before he could even see the prince. Bastián removed the pants slowly as if it pained him, certain he would hear the sound of disapproval.

Instead, Aito pointed to the pile of clothing, directing him to lay his pants on top. Bastián looked at him with confusion.

"I understand your fear," Aito said. "However, that is my master's decision, not mine." He motioned to the prominent ring on Bastián's hand. "I must ask you to forfeit everything."

Bastián shook his head. "If you truly understand, then you know I have to keep this."

"I told you," he replied with waning patience, "that will be Eisuke's decision. How do I know that isn't imbued with other magic? I cannot risk the prince's safety. Hand it over."

Bastián stood still, his ringed hand held tightly in his other.

Aito frowned. "I have given you enough leeway without my master's approval. Take it off or I will tell the guards to cut it off."

He feared the guards seeing him undressed more than the loss of a finger. Still, he hesitated. "When you say 'favored,' what do you mean? Favored how?"

"His reasons change with each one. But you may not need to worry. If you continue to refuse to comply with my request for that ring, I will consider you a threat and call the guards back."

It'd be worse for him if that happened. He didn't need to think too long to know that. He could keep refusing, fight the guards, lose that outnumbered battle, and face whatever repercussions were in store—death being the least of his worries—he could hand over his ring and then…. He didn't know what he'd do after that, but compliance was the smarter decision.

He took it off, flinching as he did so. He'd worn it for so long he could still feel its phantom weight on his finger as he handed it to Aito with one last forlorn expression. Satisfied, the older man motioned to the water. Bastián stepped in and bathed.

Once he dressed, Aito led him to his room. It was small, almost miniscule, but it was for one person. Just him. He gulped involuntarily. He really was a favored servant. Aito left, telling him he would receive instructions the following day.

Bastián sat on the meager bedding and despondently looked at his hand. The ring's absence felt so surreal. A pale band of skin encircled his finger where it used to be. He hadn't been without it since his early teenage years. He didn't know what would happen now. With head in hands, he sobbed. Of course, they wouldn't have allowed him to keep the one thing he truly needed. It had been stupid to try. He should have accepted death. That's what his life would be without it. Worse than death. At least, had he let the guards kill him, he'd have died as himself.

The door opened, and Bastián quickly hid his tears. Someone—not Aito—entered and placed a board next to his bedside. It held tea and a fragrant broth alongside a bowl of rice. The servant did not attempt any conversation and barely looked at the new resident. A simple note rested next to the plate.

I won't be there to greet you but will return in a week. I told the guards not to be rough with you. Apologies if they were. —E.

What a strange note to give your newest prisoner. Bastián calmed as much as he could. Okay. Perhaps he could take advantage of this situation. Play nice with the prince. Find out where the guards kept the personal belongings. Sneak in and take it back. That was first priority. Then he could figure out how to escape.

The simple but refreshing smell made his stomach growl. He ate, trying to settle on a plan. He had just three and a half weeks before....

At least he had made it to the palace grounds. He could impress the emperor by finding the rumored demon and be rewarded with freedom. But if he couldn't get his possessions back by then, it would matter little. At the end of that time, if it came to that, he'd force an escape. He hadn't much control when he was in that state, but thought he could focus on a simple goal. Escape the walls that caged him. Even wild animals understood that want.

CHAPTER 4

Bastián kept expecting to be shackled, abused, or—at the very least—harassed. He'd catch a glance from the house servants as if they were gawking at an exotic animal. He wondered if it was simply because he was a foreigner. Maybe it was just his eyes. He hoped it wasn't because they knew what he kept hidden.

His tasks were common household or garden chores. He learned that this garden, as beautiful as it may be, was only a subsection of the greater landscaping within the palace's walls. It had been given to prince Eisuke and his quarters were connected to it. Despite detesting the privileges that came with royalty, Bastián had lived comfortably himself. He had experience tending to his family's personal garden of natural—and sometimes supernatural—flora used in hunter practices. Although that had been more analysis than upkeep. Still, he felt more comfortable with the garden work.

Bastián saw only a few other servants during his workdays. His hunter instinct prompted him to query them, but they were terse in their replies. All responses were positive toward the prince, but it was clear they did not like Bastián's interrogation. After several attempts to source information—on the land, the royal family, or the prince himself—he noticed fewer of them out in this section of garden that he had inadvertently claimed. He was reluctant to be offended by avoidance though. He thought the cats and dogs that wandered the grounds better company anyway.

Bastián saw the prince on his third day working the garden. The note had said a week, but there was the emperor's son, reading at a stone table by the pond. He did not wear the military uniform he had the day they met. Instead, he wore a fine flowing kimono colored a pale lavender that was tailored to fit his thin frame. His hair was just the same, though. Tied back with wisps escaping the band's hold. Bastián had thought him ghoulish when he first saw him, but without the guise of military garb, the young noble appeared very delicate. Fragile, almost. Bastián turned to leave without disturbing him, but his presence had already been noticed.

"You," Eisuke said, gesturing with his hand, "come here."

Bastián approached and stood a few feet from him, head down. He heard a soft thump and looked up to see Eisuke giving him a warm smile and patting a spot across from him. He sat, uncertain what reaction he should have, his own or one proper of a servant to the prince.

The prince touched a hand to his chest, straightening as he did so. "I, as you know, am Eisuke, prince of Yasunai. Now, your introduction."

"You don't know my name?"

"No," he said. "I asked if the other servants could tell me but turns out they have been calling you 'the hunter.'"

"Charmed," he said drily. "It's Bastián."

The prince put a pale hand over his mouth and chuckled. "They didn't speak highly of your friendliness either."

Because I'm not going to stay, Bastián thought. It was useless to befriend those unimportant to his goals. Either he would find this demon and gain his freedom or take out any who'd try to stop his escape.

"Bastián," Eisuke murmured as if the sound pleased him. "I was hoping to see you."

"You were?"

"At some point," he said with a shrug. "Was told you work in the garden around this time so here I am. Just in case we crossed paths. Today we have."

"If you desire to see me, you could call on me. I am your servant."

"I don't like doing that," he said, disinterested. "Besides, I was on assignment. I have just now returned."

"Your estimate was off by four days."

"My estimate? Oh, yes. The note I gave you." Eisuke sighed. "I was too optimistic when I wrote that. I thought I could join my brothers in a training exercise. I didn't last very long."

Bastián didn't doubt that. He was more surprised that he lasted three. This prince looked like a single day of structured exercise would have been too difficult.

"You don't sound like the son of a feared emperor who kills or enslaves any outsider who sets foot within the border."

Eisuke winced. "The order I create here is not reflective of the disorder my family seeks to contain out there. That is all I will say on it. Be ungrateful if you wish, but do not voice it to the person who decided to spare and house you."

Bastián clenched his fist reflexively. This man acted as if he was a gentle savior. It infuriated him that no other servant felt as he did. He was here on a mission, and he was better than this. He was supposed to be.

"Is something wrong?" Eisuke asked, studying his demeanor.

"I am your prisoner, and yet you act as if this is a sanctuary. You sentenced my companions to death and enslavement. Yet you are brazen enough to tell me to be grateful?!"

"You truly believe you are a prisoner?" he asked with surprise. "If that's how you feel, I apologize. That is not my intention for any of my servants."

Bastián risked a severe glare. "That's it?"

Eisuke nodded solemnly. "I don't want to keep anyone against their will. If you spoke with the others, then you know they felt threatened by their prior circumstances. You say I act like this is a sanctuary. I do so because it is." He turned his head from him. "But if you are dissatisfied here, I ask that you stay for another week so that I may try to convince you otherwise. After that, please say the word, and I will assure your leave."

Bastián bit his tongue to keep from demanding he do it now. The prince had overestimated how much he had spoken to the other servants, but, if true, would explain the positive response. This man was complicated, but so was Bastián's situation. Even if forcefully taken, he had made it inside the emperor's palace. He had three weeks to find this demon, or his decision would be made for him.

"Why did you spare me?" he asked with impatience.

"I recognized your family crest."

"I'm not arrogant enough to believe that a country across an ocean knows my name."

"I didn't. I said your crest, not your name. We understand how to handle our own spirit infestations. We don't need foreign assistance." Eisuke sighed. "But inevitably they get sent here anyway. Misguided altruism or perverted sport hunting. Naturally we have records of the guilds we've come across. Since I'm only allowed on reconnaissance missions, I've studied what, and whom, I may encounter."

"How many of them have you sent to death?"

Eisuke gave a non-committal shrug. "A few here. A few there. Depends how much of a fight they put up."

"You call what we did putting up a fight?"

He laughed lightly as if a greater expression would tire him. "No, but we come back around to how I recognized your crest. The records we have say your guild is particularly ruthless and cannot be trusted to respect our ways. Your crest is mentioned as one of its founders. I couldn't risk it, you understand."

"Then it doesn't make any sense to spare *me* out of them all."

"You understand beasts. Wouldn't you agree a wolf separated from its pack is far less intimidating? And, well, if we needed leverage, you'd be the most likely prisoner anyone would care about. Even if you're not a prisoner. Exactly. Is that sufficient?"

Bastián gritted his teeth. He couldn't find fault in his logic. "I suppose it is."

"Something is still strange to me, though. I reread our information on your guild. Our records aren't current, naturally, but we have significantly fewer records of anyone named Asturias participating in hunts than we do of the other founders' lines. At least of late. I'd taken that to mean your line had died out."

Bastián shot him a glare. The guild had punished his father but hadn't ostracized him completely. "Your information is wrong. My father has been a part of our guild as long as I can remember. He's our top scholar."

Eisuke studied him with a shrewd look. "Scholar? Well, that may explain it. Although it doesn't fit with what I read. According to the history we know, the Asturias family were the most brutal hunters of them all. They encouraged eradication instead of management. It's your family that made my father particularly wary of outsider's tactics."

"That's not true at all. My father doesn't agree with eradication. Not without all the information. He's even argued with the other founders about it."

"I admitted the records were old," Eisuke said. "The last recorded hunt by your family had to be at least ten years ago, but it could be more. Say, around twenty to twenty-five. Maybe *something* changed around then. Plenty of grisly details before that, though."

Bastián held his tongue, not wanting to give in to the insufferable prodding. The young noble noticed.

"I'm going to give you the records to look over. I'd be curious your thoughts after reading them."

His soothing tone calmed Bastián's reflexive anger. "You truly mean that, don't you?"

"Why wouldn't I?"

"You would trust my word over your records?"

"I'll make my own decision on whether to trust you. But I admit that I don't know the full story. That's obvious. However, I'm more curious if *you* do. The man you speak about doesn't match the one I've read of. A new perspective, though, can change a person. Perhaps your father then. Perhaps *you* now."

Bastián decided not to argue. He would read the accounts and see how true they were. For now, he continued to glare at the prince in silence.

"That's enough of that," Eisuke said as if Bastián had spoken. "There is something more important to ask you."

"Then ask it."

"Is there anything you need?"

Bastián looked at him baffled and didn't reply.

"My men are indifferent to personal possessions. It's not my way to be as cruel about it. Mind you, I won't give back any invocating device or other weaponry, but if they took from you something you rather not go without, this is your chance to get it back."

All the fear and anxiety he had felt for the past week nearly broke through his composure.

"A ring," he said in one exhale. "It's covered in runes. It'll be obvious which one it is."

"It'll be waiting for you when you return to your room." Eisuke's mouth twitched in severe annoyance. "I sincerely apologize that you had to wait this long. The guards failed to convey the message until I returned."

What message? Bastián felt a common, but deep, fear twist inside him. It couldn't be *that*. He wouldn't still be here if it was, much less treated with any kind of dignity, no matter how shallow Bastián thought the prince's words were.

He returned to his room to see the promise fulfilled. On top of a stack of parchment—the records—was his ring. He slipped it on. The runes briefly flashed a red light. They were activated. He stared at it on his hand, trying to suppress all his emotions in losing it and then getting it back. A tear slipped from his eye and then another.

He cried in relief and felt whole again.

CHAPTER 5

Bastián studied the accounts Eisuke had given him. They didn't contain anything he hadn't read in a more boastful way before. He knew of his guild's reputation. He saw his grandfather's name mentioned frequently. He hadn't met the old curmudgeon of a man. He had died in a raid when Bastián was young. Good riddance to him from what Bastián knew of the violent elder Asturias.

He did, unfortunately, read his father's name more often than he wanted to. It was seldom by comparison and had stopped appearing around when Eisuke had said it did. Bastián was comfortable thinking of his father as the reserved scholar he knew. It didn't surprise him he had practiced the tactics his own father had taught him before transitioning to an academic role. That didn't mean Bastián ever enjoyed facing that truth, however, and that shame expressed as annoyance he took out in his chores giving an extra violent yank to weeds or a repeated stiff sweep to one corner.

Despite the other servants' aloofness towards him, Bastián was content to have the palace dogs and cats accompany him. Bastián had become accustomed to a few that particularly liked this garden. Usually, dogs raised their hackles around him before accepting or turning from his presence. These dogs, small with thick fur, could be won over by a particularly juicy slice of meat and a good scratch behind the ears.

The cats treated him as one of their own, following him as he did his chores or curling next to him when he took a break. Bastián did find it interesting they all had stumpy or bobbed tails.

He realized how easy it would be to settle into a routine here at the palace. Wake, have his meager yet filling meal, do light work in the garden, relax with the cats, and retire for the night with some reading materials. He hazarded a guess the young prince would get any records or accounts he asked for, aside from intimate family details. He regretted not asking for his personal notebook when the prince had given him the chance. He supposed he would just have to start a new one.

Midday, Bastián was unsurprised to see the prince walk gracefully to the table they had met at the other day. This, too, Bastián realized could become routine. Without needing more than a nod, he approached the noble.

"Did you receive your ring?" Eisuke asked as he sat with him.

Bastián lifted his hand. "Yes, Thank you."

The prince smiled, relieved. "What of our records? Did you have a moment to read them?"

Bastián nodded. Eisuke stared at him expectedly.

"Okay, well, what did you think?"

"I think it's easy to reach the conclusion you did."

"Which part?"

Bastián crossed his arms. "That we are a vile band of malcontents."

"Is it false?"

"Regrettably, it isn't. But I maintain I wasn't taught to be that way."

Eisuke huffed arrogantly. "Wasn't it you who barged into unknown territory with a team of skilled hunters ready to eradicate every yokai you came across?"

Bastián sighed. "No matter how it ended, being a hunter has been my whole life. I want to be back out there helping others."

"Helping?" Eisuke asked. "Is that your belief?"

"Yes. I—sometimes. Sometimes we…we are wrong."

Eisuke relaxed in his seat. "I never understood why hunters use the tactics they do. We have our own exorcists, of course, but this desire to seek out and destroy, even when the entity poses no threat, seems so self-righteous."

"I don't do that!" Bastián protested. "I know others who do, but I always hated the way those in my guild treated it like a sport. I try to respect these creatures and understand why they do what they do before cutting them down. Would anyone blame a wolf for attacking the man who provoked it? Why, then, do we blame these monsters for acting the same?"

Eisuke eyed him steadily. "You're not like most other hunters, are you?"

"I—I'm not," he said, calming down. "I try to study more than hunt. I even prayed to the gods of this land before embarking. Asked them for a safe journey. My crew ridiculed me for it. I guess they were right to. Nothing listened to my prayers."

"But they did listen," Eisuke said.

Bastián held up his arms and gave him a look of disbelief.

Eisuke took one of his hands in his own. "They granted safety to you." He spoke earnestly. "Only you."

Bastián didn't take his hand from Eisuke's clammy hold. Instead, he looked up into those red-black eyes, searching for any ulterior motive.

"Is that why you brought me here?" Bastián said, hiding his annoyance at the prince's overly friendly attitude. "A will of your gods?"

"Why is it you prayed to them? To gods not your own."

"I always do," Bastián said, taking his hand back. "If any divine spirits are to protect me, it would be the ones my bounty believes in."

"Is that something your guild practices?"

"No. Just me. The others cling to their crosses and rosaries and holy water. As if entities who had never heard of their god would give a damn about that."

"Forgive me, but it sounds like you might not give a damn about your god."

"I don't have one. I did. Once. Not anymore."

"Why is that?"

"Because I was taught he didn't give a damn about me."

Eisuke nodded solemnly. He studied his tanned skin. "I thought your race believed in the spirits and didn't confine your god to a cathedral."

"In the past we did. But look at my eyes. It wasn't just the gods that were replaced."

"Which one?"

"Which—what?"

"Which eye. Your blue or yellow one?"

Bastián tried to shake his disbelief at the question. "Either. Or both. It doesn't matter for my point."

"You mourn a dying culture."

"I mourn dying people," Bastián corrected. "My father encouraged me to spend my time in books but did warn me of both truths and lies I may find. Regardless, I was afraid of losing the knowledge of my mother. So, I studied his family's accounts of her people. They were horrible reads. Made me wonder why he'd take her as a wife if that's what those seeking conquest thought of her people. But they provided some knowledge. More importantly, they opened me up to study the accounts of other cultures. And to know how to spot when ignorance is written on the page."

"I assume your mother is no longer living."

"She died when I was a child. My father raised me, imparting what he learned from his time with her people." He reflexively ran one of his fingertips along his ring. "I know now what you were implying. Back when we first spoke. You think my father changed after he met my mother."

"I thought it a possibility."

Bastián didn't look up at him. "My father always cared for me. He always told me not to judge so quickly. To thoroughly investigate any case before using violent tactics. To try to evaluate all perspectives." He stopped spinning his ring. "His people—those who pushed themselves into my mother's land—they killed her. They burned the whole village. That was the truth he warned me about."

"I'm sorry," Eisuke said.

"There's nothing for you to be sorry about," he spat. "It doesn't affect you. This kind of experience never has and never will."

Eisuke sat quietly a few moments and then spoke softly. "I understand why you don't view my actions as kind. You don't think I can truly empathize with those I aid. You're not wrong, but I am trying. That's more than I can say about the others in my family."

Bastián shook his head. "Don't compare yourself to your brothers. Compare yourself to those outside these walls. Better than nothing is not an impressive feat. Don't aim to be better than the people who don't care. Aim to be on par with those who do."

They sat in silence for over a minute. Bastián soon took his eyes from the hurt countenance on the prince's face. It wasn't his responsibility to absolve anyone of the guilt they felt over their easy life. Especially not as a captive servant, no matter how much worse he could have been treated.

Eisuke finally spoke, talking slowly. "You didn't kill our man, did you?"

"The scout?" Bastián shook his head. "I wanted him to relay a message to the emperor. I was writing it when he was killed. I'm guessing you already knew that, or you wouldn't have spared me."

"It was easy to tell that he had been strangled," Eisuke said. "One of your crew wore a whip at his side. Same one who was quick to blame you. My guards may have tried to discourage me for welcoming a hunter, but I knew you were being betrayed."

"Most of them were petty criminals. That one, the one you noticed, I had been warned about. He was known to do more than steal some fruit or skip a day's duties."

"I see," the prince said soberly. "You knew he planned a mutiny against you."

"I knew he wanted to be the leader. I knew he disregarded my commands and coerced others to his side. I'd be an idiot if I didn't know that." Bastián crossed his arms. "But how would you know that?"

"I had the guards listen in on their conversations and report them back to me. I had an inclination that you fell far too easily, even for an inexperienced leader. Told the guards to let me know if I had been right. Before killing or transferring them, of course."

"How do I know you're not lying to me?"

Eisuke shrugged. "I suppose you don't. I can say I've done similar with all my servants. I want to hear what they say when they think they are alone. Not every bit of gossip I take seriously, but if there is any suspicion, I have it investigated. I told you I take care in who I let stay in my father's house."

"I dedicated all this time to them only for them to want to replace me as leader."

Eisuke laughed in a small, polite way. "Dedicate? How dedicated were you to a crew you clearly disliked?"

"Disliking them individually doesn't mean I wanted the group to fail. I was dedicated to leading them in our mission. A few were skilled like me, but most had rudimentary knowledge. Even our scouts constantly failed to alert me to your traps."

"What is this about traps?" Eisuke hid another chuckle behind his hand. "The imperial army doesn't lay traps. Does it seem like we'd need to?"

"But—" Bastián stopped his protest with a realization. "I thought they were clumsy when I came across them. They were done in haste. By my crew to trap me. Why wouldn't they just kill me in my sleep?"

"I don't have an answer to that. Maybe they needed proof of the story to hand over to your guild. Maybe they feared something about you that made them think the risk of you waking wasn't worth it."

"Certain magics affect humans, though. They could have bound me that way."

"You had a skilled sorcerer with you?"

"Yes. It was—me."

"Starting to understand why they thought it might be too risky."

Bastián closed his eyes and took a slow, deep breath. "I didn't like them much, but I wouldn't have killed any of them. Wouldn't have even thought it. I still protected them. Warned them away from their own traps."

"You did what a leader should do. For whatever reason, it wasn't what they wanted."

"They didn't want to do this. They wanted to leech off weak monsters and easy bounties. I hadn't anticipated how much they'd despise me for it."

"You were the one appointed as their leader. Did they truly have the option to deny you?"

"That doesn't sound as convincing as you think when it's coming from a prince."

Eisuke gave him a soft smile. "Apologies. May I ask what exactly it is they didn't want to hunt with you? It landed you in Yasunai, so I'm curious."

"An oni," he admitted, deciding he had little need for secrecy. "Possibly infiltrating the royal family."

Without pause, Eisuke laughed heartily. "No wonder you have such an air of self-importance."

"You don't know anything about it?" Bastián asked, switching to investigative mode.

"You're serious? What a ridiculous rumor."

"It was serious enough for our guild to send me."

"They didn't send you to succeed in rooting out some invisible devil. They sent you to die. If rumors of an oni reached across an ocean, so must have our proclivity for hostility to outsiders. You were warned of that, weren't you?"

He had been. Even before the temple monk told him. The guild records may have had only a small paragraph about the region, but its words were enough to caution anyone considering a visit. Yet Bastián hadn't anticipated anything he couldn't handle. He had let his pride sway his actions, and he had arrived ill-prepared for the dangers, human and monster both.

The prince's face softened. "I'm sorry I had to do that to you and your companions. They may have wanted to kill you, but I didn't know that then. I acknowledge that. My father doesn't entrust me with much, but he entrusted me with that task. I'm under pressure to perform for him. I save who I can."

Bastián believed Eisuke's earnestness but still thought he was avoiding blame.

"You didn't act like it was against your will," Bastián said.

"I have to act like that. For your sake and mine."

"What do you mean?"

"If I appear soft, the guards report this lapse to my father. I am restricted enough as is. These assignments are the only military training I've been afforded. It's the only way I can learn the arts. And if your surviving companions thought you were escorted to a life of luxury, they'd resent you for the rest of their lives, no matter how short they may be. Once I had an angered acquaintance of a servant try to storm the palace and retaliate. Since then, I don't make my motives so clearly known."

"That's clever," he said impressed. "You're very intelligent."

"And manipulative." Eisuke winked. "Father says I get that from my mother."

Bastián eyed him carefully. There appeared to be no deceit. "I believe you even if a part of me doesn't want to. I had asked the other servants about you. From the little I got out of them, either you are a cruel master, and they fear speaking the truth, or you are the opposite. You've corroborated much of what they said, and I didn't even ask you to."

"Mm," he murmured. "It pleases me they think that of me. I aim to treat my servants well. I've been dependent on them all my life. I was taught at an early age that it is best to show my appreciation for their care."

"I'm uncertain if I would equate nobility with dependence."

"Nor would I. My disposition is weak. Has been since I was born. I cannot exert too much energy because either doing so causes severe exhaustion or I simply do not have it to begin with."

The royal clothes and proper etiquette could only do so much to hide the prince's sickly frame. Bastián had scoffed at the way the guards helped with Eisuke's physical exertion the day he was taken. He had thought him a man turned lazy by his high status. Now Bastián considered this to be no privilege or ruse. He remembered those times a cold hand touched him. It was like he had been caressed by a ghost. Bastián suppressed a shudder and continued his questioning.

"I assume that's why you've not been given any rank in the imperial army."

Eisuke nodded. "I have little formal training in the martial arts compared to my brothers. I get by when necessary, though."

"I wouldn't expect that from an heir to the throne. You may be third in line, but you are still the emperor's son."

"I am not third. I'm fourth."

"How are you fourth?"

"Birth is not a guarantee for succession. My father can choose his successor. Suaki may be younger, but he's stronger than me. He isn't constantly sick. He's been able to begin combat training and sit in on political discussions—neither of which Father permitted me to do at that age. Or even much now."

"That's an odd way to be treated."

"I'm fine with it. Honestly. I'll get land from Father, and as long as I can retain my servants, that's all I need." He glanced to the sun's position. "Even though that also gives me a more relaxed schedule, I still must be going. My exhaustion sets in heavier at night. I enjoyed our talk and will miss it, but I will sign the edicts for your release this evening if you wish. No need for you to wait."

"No," Bastián said too immediately. "I'll stay. For now. May I get more reading material?"

"Certainly. What would you like?"

"Records on how your land hunts its monsters and any bestiaries. I imagine they are much more detailed than anything I had read before coming here."

"Very well," he said. "We have several volumes on that. It should keep you entertained for as long as you like to stay. When you are ready, you may go. Though I do hope you'll remain. I'm enjoying these chats."

Eisuke smiled at him and departed. There was a gentle warmth in that expression. Bastián had noticed throughout their discussion. He didn't think it was more than simple happiness. He wondered if he could get Eisuke's guard down enough for him to allow an investigation beyond the prince's corner of the palace. The records, for now, would have to do.

CHAPTER 6

Bastián didn't think the rumor of a demonic creature was as trivial as Eisuke did. His father wouldn't have sent him to die. Had he expected Bastián to ignore his orders once they arrived and embrace freedom? No. That wasn't like his father either. There had to be some truth to the monster within these walls.

Bastián sat on his bed mat, legs crossed. He breathed in deeply and exhaled steadily. Three weeks remaining had quickly turned into two, and he could already feel something stirring deep inside him that wanted to be let out. The palace grounds might yet see two monsters if he failed at this mission.

Suppress it. He repeated this thought as he found focus. Eisuke said he'd let him leave whenever he wanted. There was no need for extra stress. As long as he could regain his possessions when he walked out, there was nothing to worry about.

Just as he felt that reassurance, he felt a crawling sensation like tiny spiders had slipped under his skin and were laying their eggs among his nerve endings. Each day dragged on and Bastián frequently checked the sun's position like the bored worker he had become. Yet at the same time, he felt an intense pressure that increased with each week that passed. Two weeks was not a lot of time for an investigation. He needed to speed the process along.

Bastián continued to accompany the prince on his mid-afternoon breaks. Most of the time, he did nothing more than sit with him as he finished his tea. When they did speak, Eisuke tried to engage him in light banter, but Bastián remained guarded.

"Your tea smells strange," Bastián told him one day. Eisuke drank the same tea each day, and each day Bastián thought the same thing. Eisuke had never offered him any. He only offered fresh tea with a much more pleasing odor.

"Oh?" Eisuke tilted the cup towards him and then set it back down without interest. "It is quite pungent. I suppose I've gotten used to it. I've been drinking it all my life."

"Ever since you were born?"

"I assume shortly after that, but otherwise, yes."

"It's medicinal then," Bastián concluded. "What is it trying to cure?"

Eisuke looked at him with slight annoyance and put a hand to his chest. "The obvious."

"Well, it doesn't seem to be having an effect."

The prince's hurt expression told Bastiánhe had been too blunt, but he only mildly regretted saying it.

"What's in it?" Bastián asked.

Eisuke looked at the cup with much less interest than Bastián. "I've never thought to ask." He set it down and pushed it to the side. "How are you liking our chats? You don't have to oblige me."

"It's oddly comforting to have someone to talk to. The other servants are wary of me. I haven't exactly been the friendliest towards them, either."

"Yes, I've been told you're quite withdrawn. I guess that means you're still uncomfortable here."

"Can you blame me for being unsettled?" Bastián said, grasping his arms. "I, regrettably, am beginning to feel grateful. I can recognize the poor position I was in. But I cannot forget how I came here or how only I was spared."

"I am sorry that happened."

"Are you? Son of an emperor who does the same?!"

"If I judged you based on what I knew of a hunter's proclivity for violence, I would have sent you with the rest of your crew. I hoped you could do the same for me."

Eisuke had spoken with the closest tone to anger Bastián had heard since arriving. He looked over to the prince. He had abandoned his poised manner and sulked in his chair, petulantly stirring his tea. Bastián didn't understand the reaction.

"I'm trying," Bastián said, questioning why he was even defending himself. "I feel conflicted."

"I haven't shown you enough kindness?" He hadn't changed positions and barely looked at him. "I hoped you could regard me as a friend."

Bastián sharply bit his tongue so he wouldn't laugh. "A friend? You are royalty, and I'm—"

"Stop thinking of me like that!" His fist hit the table in frustration, but it barely made a thud. "I'm worthless as royalty. My own line doesn't want me. My servants—everyone I've brought into this sanctuary—think of me the same. That I'm a kind, but untouchable specter!"

Eisuke panted like a dog after a run. His hair fell out of place, and he plunged one hand into it. He closed his eyes and mouth, steadily getting his breathing under control. Bastián noticed how pale that hand looked against his black hair. Pale and somewhat boney. The hand of a sickened elder, not one of a man in his prime.

"You really are weak, aren't you?" Bastián observed.

"Of course, I am," Eisuke said shortly. "I wouldn't lie about that."

Bastián's eyes fell on the teacup again. He'd have to study what was in there. He was curious what medicinal remedies this land had and even more so why it seemed to be doing so little for the prince's composition.

"Forgive me," Eisuke said, raising his head with effort. "I am tired of being dismissed when I try to relate. No one has accepted my offer of friendship. I doubt even Aito regards me as anything more than a chore he does for my father."

Bastián found it difficult to have sympathy for him. "You don't regard us as much more than pets. Feed us. Shelter us. Give us our exercise and favorite toys."

"No," Eisuke said with a rare glare in his eyes. "A dog offers protection. A cat shares its hunt. Even a bird returns to the roost despite being given the chance to fly. Humans do none of these. They give me loyalty out of fear, flattery out of hope of favors, and leave never to return when offered. I don't view them more than a pet. I view them less than one. And still, I try to offer them peace."

Bastián scrutinized the prince. He was a man who had faced little except loneliness and rejection despite his nobility.

"When you first saw me," Bastián said, "you remarked on my clothing. You knew I was of high status with or without my crest. Is that why you spared me? Truth, this time."

"I haven't lied to you," he insisted.

"But you haven't told me it in full. You thought you could relate to me."

"Where's the lie?" Eisuke asked, sounding very tired. "I was born into this status and the privileges it gives me. And yet, I feel like a disappointment to both my father and my country. Yes. I thought maybe you could relate. That we could relate together."

"You're an idealist."

Eisuke flinched as if he had been scolded. "I know. Deride me for having hope. It's not the first time."

Bastián shook his head. "I won't do that."

Eisuke perked up but did not relax. Bastián continued.

"I needed to know you weren't hiding your motives from me. Consider me cruel if you want, but I needed to get past your flowery ruse. Now we can speak more plainly with each other."

"To consider you cruel would be hypocritical of me. You have every right to be skeptical, and I apologize for not being able to diffuse that skepticism earlier."

Bastián kept his stern gaze, but inside his heart pounded against the empty spot where the metal of his necklace typically rested. His blood thumped through the capillaries on his ringed finger. He still kept things hidden from this prince. A part of him felt guilt at his own hypocrisy. But he was the prince's victim. He deserved to keep his privacy as long as he could.

"Eisuke," he said, "I will keep up appearances as your servant, but I am willing to be your friend while I am here."

Eisuke happily clasped Bastián's hands in his own oddly cold ones. "Thank you for giving me a chance."

Bastián resisted the want to roll his eyes. The prince was terribly naïve. Bastián almost felt an urge to protect him. Almost. Eisuke could wear an assortment of masks when necessary, but in his heart, he felt alone and ashamed. Bastián could pity him for the time being. He thought that proudly, ready to don his own mask.

Bastián rested on a stone ledge overlooking a small pond. His work was done, and he thought it a nice way to end his day. A cat came up to him, rubbing against his leg. He gave it a small piece of fish he had saved from his dinner. The cat grabbed it in its jaws and trotted off to eat alone as if Bastián would take it from him.

So much for a cat sharing his hunt, Bastián thought.

"Are you spoiling the palace staff?" Eisuke asked cheerfully. "He's our best rat catcher."

"Then I feel no shame rewarding him," Bastián said, shaking off the surprise at Eisuke's presence. "I thought you didn't come out to the garden this late. We can move to the table if you want."

"No need. I don't have my tea with me."

Eisuke sat next to him. Bastián noted it was the first time there hadn't been a table—or spear—separating them. The flowing robes of nobility seemed to swallow his thin frame. Bastián wondered if he felt suffocated under them.

"I missed you earlier today," Eisuke said, "so I decided on an evening stroll." Eisuke watched the cat walk back to Bastián but as soon as it spotted Eisuke, it darted under a hedge. "You seem to have an affinity toward cats."

Bastián smiled at how ironic that statement was. "Of course. They're good hunters. Something to admire about them."

Eisuke stretched his neck to see two white paws turn gray from the hedge's shadow. "That one's Makoto. He's usually not very friendly."

"Ah. I had thought to call him 'Stumpy', but all of the cats here have short tails."

"Well, we can't have any turning into a bakeneko."

Bastián nearly called out the superstition before he saw the smile Eisuke had said it with. "You don't believe that they would."

"What do you think, hunter? Haven't you encountered enough monsters to believe our stories?"

"I think every folktale starts with little bit of truth. But as it's told throughout the generations, it gets exaggerated or misinterpreted. I try to find out what that truth is before striking."

"Sounds like a strategy that would take much time. I doubt it's a popular one." Eisuke shrugged. "I don't personally believe our friends here will turn to monsters, but my father thinks it best to use extreme caution when dealing with potential yokai. He would agree with many of your guild's ways."

"That's unfortunate." Bastián leaned over and threw another piece of fish toward the hedge. A white paw popped out and dragged the fish into the shadow. "We had a cat on our ship. A dog, too. I was often the one to feed and groom them. I left them both with the dock keepers. Paid the men to care for them." Bastián sighed. "I hope they did. I miss their comfort."

"A ship cat and a dock dog are hardy workers. I'm sure they will value them, too."

"I haven't seen you with any pet at your side. Do you not like cats?" It felt so silly to ask, but Eisuke wasn't in on Bastián's secret joke.

"I do like them. They bring prosperity and are good at keeping secrets." Eisuke looked over to the hedge. The cat had retreated farther into the shrub, and he could see no trace of it. "I wish they—cats, dogs, all animals—liked me, but I've not met one that wanted to get near me. Even my brothers' dogs snarl if I get too close."

"Are horses excluded from that? Your mount didn't seem upset with you around."

"You have a vivid memory, don't you? Horses do act restless. The one I ride is very old. Too old to be bothered by whomever rides him."

Bastián suddenly felt very sad for him. He knew him to be lonely. Bastián was no stranger to that. But he had always had the company of a pet when he had no one else.

"You mention your father and your brothers frequently," Bastián said, "but I haven't heard talk of your mother."

"She's dead," Eisuke confirmed. "It happened when I was just entering adolescence. She died during Suaki's birth. You know how those things sometimes go."

"Sorry," he said.

He shrugged. "I wasn't close with her. I'm not close to any of my family. I get the sense they have disdain for me even when they do include me like I'm an embarrassment to our imperial might."

"Did she not take care of you as a child?"

He looked confused. "Oh, no. That's why I have servants. Aito has watched over me for as long as I can remember. Father actually took more interest in my care than Mother did." His tone turned solemn. "You're right, though. I have wondered why my older brothers speak of her fondly and what I missed by not knowing her. Father grieved heavily when she died. I remember him saying he had the worst luck with women and warned all his sons not to do the same. Which is easily avoidable for me."

Bastián caught the unintentional hint. Or maybe it wasn't so unintentional. He had been originally intended to be a *favored* servant, hadn't he? He had quickly forgotten about the insinuation when Eisuke gave him ample space. He briefly assessed the seated man next to him. Underweight. Slight in frame. No sign of facial hair. Little tone in his muscles. Bastián wondered what he'd look like if healthy. As he was, Bastián didn't even experience the slight jealousy he often had towards other men's physiques.

"If I left," Bastián said, "would you truly miss me?"

The prince grazed a hand across his thigh. "Yes, I would."

Bastián felt the hand on top his leg. Oh. *Oh.* That's why the prince had gotten annoyed and flustered the day before. Bastián felt a surge of inner excitement. He wished he could splash icy water on that damn beast inside him. He wouldn't even be considering returning the flirtation if it weren't getting so close to a full moon.

Bastián blamed that feral side of him for entertaining these thoughts. Eisuke just thought he liked him. If he knew—damn it. He always had to stop that kind of thinking. But there was a very real possibility any attraction Eisuke had to him would dissolve as soon as his clothes were off.

Bastián held his gaze. "Why would you miss me?"

Eisuke smiled. "I like seeing you. I like talking to you." That light touch turned firm. He leaned in. Not a lot. Just enough to be noticeable. "I like—"

Eisuke stopped suddenly as if struck blind by his own flirtation. He abruptly returned to his normal sitting position.

"I'm sorry," Eisuke said. "I should have asked. Or done nothing. I would miss you. And not just because—yeah. I think you're intelligent, and honest, and you want to do the right thing. You make for good conversation."

Bastián recognized the attempted recovery and awkward apology. He'd been the one to say the same enough in his life. He saw his commonly displaced hairs and for the first time imagined reaching out and tucking them behind the prince's ear himself. But he had to know how safe they were.

"I'm curious if your father would approve of such inclinations."

"I'm not important enough for him to care. He has three other sons to inherit the kingdom and sire themselves an heir. If I were well enough to lead an army, maybe he would care. But I mean little to him."

"Eisuke," Bastián said evenly. He watched sadly as the prince turned his tentative attention to him. "I'd be willing to return some of that affection. Not yet, but—" He chuckled to himself. "—before I leave. For sure. It can be my thanks to you."

"Oh, no, no. I don't want you to feel like you have to. It's not a debt. And even if it was, I'd not ask for it to be repaid. At all, really, but especially not that way."

Bastián stroked his cheek. "I didn't mean it like that. Promise. I know how that rejection and that fear feels."

Bastián had said not yet, but the way his finger caught a few stray strands of his fine hair and the way the prince looked near tears with gratitude made him try the hardest he could to resist kissing him. He hadn't promised sex and didn't intend to. That always held the chance of being a step too far. However, Bastián wouldn't mind some playful teasing.

"I think I should depart for now," Eisuke announced. "We can converse again. Maybe somewhere more private."

"Are you alright?" he asked, concerned.

"Yes, just—somewhere more private next time."

"Of course."

Bastián watched him retreat back to the palace as if he were ashamed. He hoped he wasn't. His compassion was limited, but if Eisuke were ashamed, he might be willing to ease that anxiety. He knew far too well the agony of such a feeling when it went unrequited. He felt a cautious excitement at the thought of pleasuring the prince. Though maybe that eagerness was just the beast stirring inside him impatient for the full moon.

CHAPTER 8

After two days passed with no request for his company, Bastián worried the prince felt too ashamed to be around him. It wouldn't have seemed so long if Bastián hadn't been counting down the days until he had to leave—or at least get his necklace back. He supposed he could stay longer if he had that, but he didn't want to get comfortable as a servant. Eisuke insisted he wasn't his captor, but he didn't feel free. He was a rat in an elaborate cage but still confined to that cage. Yet perhaps that was better than the alternative.

Bastián didn't doubt the spite his crew had had for him. He recognized Eisuke had likely thwarted his death by their hands. Now, after going over every detail of their journey in his head, he was certain they had planned to mutiny. Their carelessness got them captured and killed, not Bastián's.

His growing affection for the prince wasn't for that alone. Eisuke hadn't known all the details seeing him that day. Bastián admired his ability to make astute deductions. He had been right in many of his assumptions about him. Learning about his crew and Eisuke's kind treatment to other servants allowed Bastián to soften his criticism and let his thoughts linger on the prince more than they had. If he spoke true about letting him go whenever he wanted, then Bastián dared to soften around him even more.

He had no feelings of dread when Eisuke finally did call for him. He found himself excited to see him and surprised at how much he had missed him. The prince invited him to an enclosed sitting room. He gestured to the cushions, and Bastián took a seat at the table. He watched Eisuke's eyes dart nervously.

"I need to speak candidly with you," Eisuke said. "I won't force anything just because there is a door I can close."

Bastián's eyes fell on the pot gently boiling over the heat.

"Have you had your tea yet?"

Eisuke shook his head.

"You can talk to me while you drink. It might help us relax."

Bastián didn't feel nervous but hoped acting as if they shared the burden would help calm him. He rose and took the pot from the fire. Eisuke held his hand out for it. Bastián didn't give it to him, staring instead at the box of tea.

"I can pour my own tea," Eisuke said in jest. "You don't need to do it."

"Right," Bastián said, snapping back to attention. "Could I take some tea leaves?"

"I don't think you'd like it. It tastes how it smells."

"Not to drink."

Eisuke gripped the container protectively. "Why then?"

"Call it a hunter's instinct," Bastián said. "I'm curious about its medicinal properties if nothing else."

Eisuke hesitated, his grip briefly tightening over the box. He then scooted the container towards him. "Go ahead. I don't have anything to hide."

You really don't, do you? Bastián thought, surprised at the trust in his realization. *But someone may be hiding something from you.*

Bastián took a pinch of the leaves only to realize he had nothing to place it in. Eisuke tentatively gave him a small piece of cloth. Bastián felt sympathy for him. Eisuke must have thought of this tea as the only thing giving him as much energy as he did have. Now Bastián challenged that. Regardless, Bastián tucked the sachet into his own clothing. He'd study it when he was back in his room.

"I apologize for last time," Eisuke said, as Bastián poured hot water into his cup.

"Which part?"

"Hmm?"

"Which part do you apologize for?"

"For—for leaving as I did. I was flustered."

Bastián put a hand over his mouth to hide a smile. "And you're not now?"

"Please," he said. "You know what we—what I—almost did could endanger us. That's what I'm sorry for. I should have handled it better. Both confessing my attraction, and how I reacted when you…"

"You're not experienced with this," Bastián observed.

"How can I be? I'm the weakest son of the emperor! Servants tend to my every need, and the public's eyes are on me whenever I go out. I'm rarely alone and my chances to be with anyone outside this place are far fewer."

"You've never asked this of other servants?"

"I—yes. But only because I was trying to figure out my attractions, and I told them they didn't have to if they didn't want to."

"How do you know they didn't humor you out of obligation?"

"I don't. And they probably did. But you're not like that. You don't have any loyalty to me or this country."

"Did that factor into you sparing me?"

"No. Honest. But it's part of how I could let myself be attracted to you."

"It's okay," Bastián said. "I understand. It's hard to fall for another man when that doesn't feel safe."

Eisuke looked at him strangely. "I think I misunderstood something. What are you talking about?"

"What am I—? A man having a relationship with another man."

Eisuke laughed but stopped when he saw Bastián's severe demeanor. "Oh, you're serious. Is that…is that outlawed for you?"

"Yes! What were you talking about then?"

"That you are a servant, and I am nobility. That our classes are so far apart."

"Even when I asked if your father would approve?"

Eisuke shrugged. "Yes, same answer. If I was worth anything to him, I'm sure he'd prefer I properly marry a woman and produce an heir, but even so he wouldn't mind if I spent time with a young man before that."

"Your gods really don't care?"

"Why would they? They are concerned about spiritual dedication not the physical body. Do your gods care? The ones you used to follow, that is."

"Yes, they care a lot. It'd make you a social outcast at best and kill you at worst."

"That's stupid."

"I don't disagree. It's why I stopped following them. It's just—I didn't expect this."

"Do your religious leaders expect groups of men, away from women for long periods of time, to never have sex with each other?"

"They…they have a lot of teachings that don't make much sense."

"Well," Eisuke said, pushing aside his humor, "I'm sorry you've had to live like that. I will say I think we are a little too role-focused when it comes to having a man as a lover, but if you feel that way or engage in it won't get you punished here."

"I'm really not used to that."

Eisuke grasped Bastián's arm. "I can't change how we met, and I can't express how sorry I am about that. I wanted to give you a chance our guards wouldn't. I know what it's like to fail in the eyes of your father and country. I kept myself distant to see if my attraction to you was purely physical. It isn't, and I can't hide that anymore."

"You don't have to. Truly, I understand what it's like to be forced to hide your feelings."

Eisuke let go and turned his eyes from him. "I am being rather myopic. I have lived with much greater privilege than you. Yet I'm complaining about my lack of romantic partners."

"I'm unsure if this will make you feel better, but I may be even less experienced than you."

"In what way?"

"Well, it's rather embarrassing, but I've not had sex before."

"Never?"

He nodded. "Kissed, made out, a quick grope—that's all I've done with another. I have also masturbated. So, I'm not some untouched virgin down there."

"That isn't an issue for me."

Bastián gave him a shrewd glance. Such a princely thing to say. "I didn't tell you because I thought I needed to have some sort of chastity for you to consider a relationship with me."

Eisuke shook his head, face flushed. "It was an unintentional response. Forgive me. I'm surprised. You don't seem prudish."

"I'm mostly around haughty, religious hunters. Didn't particularly find anyone worth that risk."

"I hope you don't feel that way with me."

Bastián smiled. "I thought myself dead when we first met. And, in truth, a part of me does feel like it died that day. I feel very separate from that hunter who was determined to find a monster. In a way it feels freeing to lose that part of me."

Eisuke looked at him with sadness. He must have noticed that the strained attempt at amusement had shifted to sorrow. "Don't lose yourself. Please. Leave before that happens. I had to intervene because you were trespassers, not because you were hunters. I have no ill will towards your profession. I do think maybe you should alter your tactics or leave it to the exorcists who know better, but you weren't captured because you were a hunter. You made me think differently about them, in truth."

Bastián looked up at him with a pleading look. "How so?"

"I thought all foreign hunters were disrespectful towards our customs and too arrogant to think they shouldn't be. You impressed me not only with your knowledge, but that you do seek to respect the land's traditions and its residents, human and monster both."

"You praise me too much," Bastián said with a quiver in his voice. "It's an assignment, and everything I did was in pursuit of that. I hadn't given up on that thinking until recently. But I'm glad I can now show you something beyond that."

Eisuke leaned in, placing a hand on his arm. Their eyes met. He leaned closer. Yet he did nothing, only gazed longingly at him.

"It's okay," Bastián said. "You may."

"I may what?"

"Kiss me."

Bastián trailed a hand up his arm and encouraged him to lean closer. Eisuke smelled of sweet oils and perfumes, but his lips tasted acrid. No doubt from the tea. Yet Bastián felt a strong pull towards him. One he couldn't fully blame on his heightened senses. His rational brain thought he was simply humoring the idea. It could be something fun, something memorable, before he took the prince's offer to leave.

Bastián felt him try to end it as a quick, chaste kiss. Bastián plunged his hand into his hair and held him close. He used his surprise to slide his tongue into his mouth. Bastián wasn't going to let him get away with his princely etiquette. That sour, coppery taste was stronger, yet he didn't mind it. He felt odd ridges on the side of his head as he massaged his scalp. He mentally filed it away to review later.

Bastián felt a hand on his chest, a tentative one that asked for a pause rather than an increase in tension. All the anxiety beforehand must have taken its toll on Eisuke's exhaustion. Bastián shifted his weight back to his knees and caught sight of the prince straining to catch his breath.

"My disposition," he explained. "I'm feeling exceptionally weak. Trust that I'm just as disappointed as you, but I don't want to pass out in the middle of this."

"I'll return to my other tasks, then." He kissed his hand. "Rest well."

They departed, and Bastián finished his daily chores. In undressing for the night, the tea leaves fell out of his pocket. Bastián had nearly forgotten he had taken some. He studied them and recognized about half the ingredients, but the rest were native to this land. He had a further investigation to do before he could form any conclusion.

Five days passed. Bastián was uncertain he even wanted to complete the mission anymore. He blamed his instincts, senses, and feral beast for getting too excited over one sensual kiss. Usually, he could make use of his heightened senses—a few days of extensive study with little sleep, increasing the intensity of his training regimen, or trying, but usually failing, to find a colleague who wasn't scared to flirt with another man. But here, he didn't have his typical outlets.

As much as his body wanted more, his mind needed to be comfortable with the noble prince who had captured him. Bastián was mindful of Eisuke's disposition both in regard to his health and his nervousness about the relationship. They did little more than touch each other or share a sly kiss when in private.

"You seem restless," Eisuke observed one day.

"I have to admit this lifestyle doesn't stimulate me as my previous one did. All the years of honing my skills…. I feel rather useless here."

Eisuke turned solemn. "Are you going to leave soon?"

Bastián shook his head. "I'm still undecided." He smiled to himself. "You've made it enticing to stay."

Eisuke thought for a moment. "You could accompany me on a trip outside the palace."

"That wouldn't be too suspicious?"

"Why would it? Surely the emperor's most fragile son would

have several servants wherever he went."

"You don't already?"

"I do. Hence no one would suspect anything. We also wouldn't go far. There are precautions we should take. Walk beside me, avert your gaze unless spoken to, and no touching. My brothers jest enough that I use my servants for sexual endeavors, even before it was true."

Bastián hoped he was referring to their relationship.

"When can we do this?"

"We can go today, if you would like. You can accompany me to the nearest temple."

As soon as Eisuke had finished his afternoon serving of special tea, they ventured out. They didn't change attire: Bastián remained in his servant robes and Eisuke in his ill-fitting kimono. Eisuke walked slowly and carefully. Bastián was still surprised this was the same man who commanded his crew to perish, albeit he certainly hadn't studied him nearly as much as he had by now.

They passed through the palace's exquisite gardens. Bastián tended only to a section of them. He admired the red bridges and stone lanterns and listened to calm waters of the pond with the koi carp snapping at insects on the surface. He understood why Eisuke spent much of his time here. It was the most peaceful place inside the palace walls.

Bastián could tell Eisuke wanted to engage him in conversation but had to resist as he led him outside the gates. Bastián had landed in this country during the summer. Now autumn had set in. The trees had turned a vibrant red and yellow that contrasted against the evergreen shrubbery.

They reached the temple, and Eisuke asked him to wait outside as he went in.

"I worry our kami may not understand why I bring a foreigner who hunts them into their sacred place."

Bastián nodded in understanding, keeping his responses to a minimum. Even if it had lacked conversation, Bastián appreciated the walk outside the palace.

He did feel awkward standing outside the temple as the prince performed his prayers. His eyes wandered and fell on a fox a few yards away. It sat perfectly still with its bushy tail wrapped around its feet. He thought it strange a fox would watch them as closely as this.

He took a cautious step towards it. It didn't move yet blinked at him, acknowledging the approach. When he was almost close enough to touch it, it sprinted behind the stone wall. Bastián started to turn away, but curiosity urged him forward instead. He placed a hand on the cool stone expecting to see the playful fox eager to continue the chase.

What he didn't expect to see was an elegant and poised woman with the furry ears and tail identical in color to the fox he had followed. She smiled at him with sharp canines. A kitsune.

"I assume you know why I wanted your attention," she said.

Bastián shook his head. "I'm afraid I don't."

"A beastly hunter escorting a frail prince. You're a rare sight."

Bastián pursed his lips. His ordinary gray servant clothing should have disguised his identity as a hunter. But that was only effective on humans. Certain spirits could see past that. Usually the powerful and cunning ones. He had read how kitsunes could be tricksters. He didn't need one to be coy with him.

"Is that all?" he asked. "I grow tired of this land and its spirits wanting to point out things I already know."

"But there is something you don't know, isn't there?" She giggled. "You even brought it with you."

Tea leaves. He had taken them in case he could sneak some purifying oil from the shrine. He took out the sachet, and the kitsune immediately sniffed the air.

"Ah," she said. "The smell of blood. And from my fox friends' favorite prey."

Bastián recalled the summer his father tried to keep chickens but a non-stop battle against foxes taking the weakest of the flock drove him to quit the endeavor. It didn't help that his young child thought the vulpines cute and was faced with a tearful boy anytime he shot one.

"Chicken?" he guessed.

She nodded. "Rooster, specifically, but close enough."

"Can you determine what else is in it?"

He took a step closer to her, sachet outstretched. She leaned back with an upturned nose.

"Other things much less pleasant to smell," she said. "But why ask when you already know?"

"Suppression material."

"And an added enchantment for assurance."

He looked down at the packet of leaves. "But why?"

"Oh, you are not that dumb, little hunter."

He frowned. "Why tell me this? Answer that."

She shrugged and gave him another toothy smile. "Your prince is very naïve. You are not." She touched the air as if thrumming a string. "I like to pull at threads when I see them."

He recalled the monk mentioning a thread. "Why give this tea to him? Is it harming him?"

She cocked her head, debating her response. "Harming, no? Sustaining? Barely. That's why he's weak."

"You know him then?"

She gestured to a stone statue of a fox. "We are spirits of Inari. I have watched him pray many times. He is rather a curious thing, don't you agree?"

"But he doesn't know that he is."

She laughed behind a polite hand. "Of course not. His family couldn't have power over him if he knew."

Bastián didn't think this exchange was humorous and kept a rigid stance. She either found all human matters amusing even if it involved yokai or she was pleased at her deception. Yet all his evidence supported the same conclusion. He would have been excited by that a month ago. Now, he felt a lump of dread in his stomach at the thought.

"How has an oni been kept within the royal family?"

"Little hunter, you know well of curses. His father felled a monster or two in his day just like you. One sought revenge for her mate, tricked him, and Eisuke was born. She used the paternal link to steal life from the emperor. Twenty-five years he must be kept alive, or the emperor would lose those years himself."

Bastián realized he didn't actually know how old Eisuke was. "How close is he to that deadline?"

She giggled. "About the same as you are to your own. After that day, the curse on the emperor is no more. You know what that means."

"He will be free to kill his son without repercussion."

"Might you pray this prince's life is never an inconvenience to the dear emperor and perhaps he'll be spared. Regardless, the emperor will have difficulty extinguishing him completely."

"I thought onis were less spiritual in form than other yokai."

"Not this one. His mother used blood to bind father and son. Blood to sustain his body, and blood to siphon the energy of age."

"He's a blood demon then."

She nodded. "Which is why his life has been sustained by the tea but has not flourished from the scraps of dried livestock within it."

Bastián found his breath caught in his throat.

"I need proof," he said, his body finally forcing him to realize the tension he had over his uncertainty.

"Is my word not proof enough?" she said, grinning. She pointed to an asagao flower at her feet. "Take the petals of the flower that blooms on autumn mornings. It will dispel any illusion. Only for you, and only for a moment."

"Thank you," he said.

She closed her eyes and gave a small bow. As she rose, he saw one of her long ears perk up and twitch in the direction of the shrine.

"You should hurry back, little beastie. Your prince is almost finished with his prayers."

He glanced at the shrine then back at the woman. She was a fox again. She gave him an amused nod then darted into the forest as Bastián knelt to quickly gather the flowers.

He returned to the shrine steps just as Eisuke exited the small building. He apologized for taking so long, and they began their walk back to the palace. Bastián thought he appeared troubled. The kitsune had called him naïve and, by his own admission, he seldom had romantic relationships. He must be doing his best to calm his nerves around him.

They were at the outer garden when Bastián placed a hand on his chest, stopping him. All the restlessness of the prior weeks breached the surface, and he felt a sudden excitement. Bastián wanted to curse the moon, but he knew he couldn't. Even with the moon near its peak, he couldn't lie to himself anymore that the prince intrigued him. More than intrigued. A dangerous feeling to pursue, but one that he could not ignore. Nor did he want to ignore it.

They kissed and when they parted, Bastián stared into those earnest and nervous blood-red eyes. Everything the kitsune said was true. He had known it deep down. Eisuke was a monster. His monster. The very one he'd been sent to kill.

He guided Eisuke to sit and then knelt in front of him. He ducked his head under his robes and took him into his mouth. He took him deep, massaging his cock with his throat muscles and pressing his compressed tongue against him as best he could. Even sitting, Eisuke leaned over him, breathing heavily and stroking the top of his head. Bastián knew not to push his frail composition too far but at the same time, he wanted to give him a pleasure he wouldn't soon forget.

Eisuke came into his mouth just as exhaustion hit him. He leaned against the garden wall, placing a hand on it for extra support as Bastián released his mouth. He took a seat next to him, fixing Eisuke's clothing for him.

As he gazed at his partner's contented face, Bastián tried to visualize horns, sharp teeth, and gray, stretched skin. It'd be odd for him to lose his delicate features. But that wasn't his true self. He wasn't truly the waif-like son of an emperor. He was a fearsome beast. Just like Bastián was.

"You're telling me you hadn't done that before?" Eisuke said.

Bastián kissed him, sharing his salty taste. "Oh, that I've done. Sharing my own body with another—that's what eludes me."

Eisuke opened his mouth to say something but decided against it. He squeezed Bastián's hand instead. Bastián found his uncertainty wholly endearing. He could act like the callous soldier when given an order, but he was a sheltered prince unknowing of the true power he held. Bastián hoped to show that power to him and break the magical chains that had been placed upon him.

CHAPTER 10

Bastián wanted to thoroughly study the prince's body. For hunter reasons, he told himself. To see if the kitsune had told him the truth. That was all.

Bastián proposed a massage which Eisuke readily accepted. He asked to have time to prepare and was granted access to a private room. Bastián placed the flowers he had taken from the shrine into a bottle and let the blooms infuse the oil. He smelled the resulting tincture. It reminded him of lavender. He doubted Eisuke would think anything was suspect.

After he had finished setting up, Eisuke entered and knelt on the futon. He stripped off his robe and covered his waist with a modest towel. Bastián pretended to be busy with the oils as not to seem like he was intentionally staring. The clear glass of the bottles gave him a decent view. For whatever reason his favorite part was watching Eisuke's naked frame redo the tying of his long ponytail. He always tried to tame his hair, but always some strands fell loose. It was the one bit of impropriety he couldn't suppress.

Bastián started with the flower-infused oil. He rubbed it over Eisuke's shoulders. He followed the muscles along his spine. His boney, pronounced spine. Bastián felt disgust well up in him. Not for Eisuke but for the treatment he received. Starving a monster to keep it weak was a basic, but cruel, tactic. Easy to do if the creature was ensnared. Eisuke was kept prisoner by his ignorance.

The enchanted oil worked quickly. Bastián could see as if staring into two worlds. One was the prince he knew. The other had gray skin and white hair. Two reddish brown horns grew from his head. His fingers and toes were elongated to better grip and scratch at his victims. Each ended in sharp talons matching the color of his horns. Eisuke opened his eyes at the pause, and Bastián saw them as bright red irises with a slit pupil set against black sclera. He had just enough time to mentally categorize all the changes before the vision faded.

"Anything wrong?" Eisuke asked.

"No, no," Bastián said quickly. "I haven't done this before. Deciding the best way."

"You're doing fine by me," he said, resting his head back down on the pillow. "I'll let you know if you're not."

Bastián continued his examination, keeping the image of his demonic form in his mind. He prodded his calves and rubbed his feet. His legs were thin, but not as underdeveloped as his hands. He was able to walk and ride fine, after all. Stiffness in his neck and shoulders, but he did spend most of his day reading. Nothing unusual, and reactions seemed normal. Surprisingly to Bastián, he could not find evidence of old injuries or previous breaks that may not have healed well. He found that both a relief and moderately depressing. Eisuke certainly hadn't been physically abused, but his body showed little sign of having lived an active life. No scars from childhood falls or tired muscles from martial training. Bastián's own body was dotted with scars of all sizes and shapes from various monsters and general hazards of the job.

Bastián moved his hand to Eisuke waist, spreading his fingers so his thumbs could press into the small of his back. Eisuke arched his back, pushing his hips against the futon. He rotated his hands, caressing the top curve of his ass.

Eisuke let out a little moan and turned his head to the side. Bastián could see his face starting to flush. Bastián liked when he did that but did wonder how much was because of his weak constitution rather than arousal.

"Turn your hips to the side," Bastián instructed.

"What are you going to do to me, good hunter?"

Bastián felt paralyzed for a moment hearing Eisuke call him that. A beast calling him a good hunter. He liked hearing it.

"Trust a hunter's instincts," he said, leaning over him to whisper it in his ear.

Eisuke smiled in response and turned on his side. Bastián covered his hand in the oil. He massaged the gluteus muscles, running his hand between them. He stroked his hole, felt his sphincter relax, and inserted first one then two fingers inside him.

Eisuke gripped the pillow tightly as Bastián worked his fingers in and out of him. His knuckles grazed his prostate, and he held his hand for a few seconds each time, mimicking a deep thrust. Eisuke was certainly red in the face now and breathing heavily. The tip of his penis leaked precum. Bastián grasped it with his other hand, moving along the shaft in time with the one in his ass.

Eisuke's whole body curled in on itself as he ejaculated onto the sheets. He panted, and Bastián slowly removed his hand, replacing the towel over his waist. He wiped his hands and leaned over Eisuke. He grasped the hair sticking to his sweaty face, making sure to caress the ridges on his skull as he pulled it back. It had become a favorite of his.

"Thank you," Eisuke said.

"You're welcome," Bastián said, kissing him on the cheek.

"When—when I have strength, you'll have to teach me how to do similar for you."

Bastián continued stroking his hair as he slowly drifted to sleep. When he eyes closed, he let his frown show. Had he truly let himself believe this demon was the victim in all this? He had, and he had done so willingly. After all his years nose deep in books, he had promised himself never to hunt and kill a monster that was not truly monstrous. Bastián himself was one of those monsters. Many would kill him simply for existing, necklace or not. He hadn't ever expected to know another like himself, intimately or casually, but he had to admit he wasn't fighting those feelings. What he saw in the vision hadn't scared him. It was still Eisuke, and he still cared about him.

Bastián woke to find an invitation along with his breakfast. His heart fluttered seeing the elegant *E*. Eisuke requested his company at a festival that night. Under the tray was a yukata for him to wear. Bastián could hardly contain his excitement as he did his daily tasks.

That evening, Bastián was greeted by Aito, ready to escort him to the prince. The old servant was as stoic as the day Bastián arrived at the palace.

"You have gotten comfortable here, hunter," Aito stated as Bastián followed him.

"I wouldn't say that," Bastián protested.

"Excuse me," Aito said. "May I say instead that you have gotten comfortable with the prince."

Bastián didn't reply, unsure what, if anything, the older man wanted him to confirm.

"Eisuke is excited for this," Aito continued. "More excited than I have seen him in years. Don't disappoint him. He so rarely gets these opportunities."

"I won't," Bastián said.

Aito nodded but retained a stern stare. He ushered Bastián to the outer wall of Eisuke's private garden. The prince waited there on one of the stone benches.

Eisuke jumped from his seated position when he saw the pair. His stance wobbled. With a practiced stride, Aito stepped next to him, and Eisuke grabbed his arm to steady himself. He turned red with embarrassment. Bastian walked over and took Eisuke's hand from Aito.

"It's okay," Bastián said, "I'll be by his side the rest of the night."

Aito's glance remained shrewd but polite. "Do not let him overexert himself." His face softened and a small smile could barely be seen. "Otherwise, do have fun."

Aito left and Eisuke could now turn his attention to Bastián. He smiled seeing him in the festive wear.

"You look—acceptable," he said, catching himself from complimenting him within earshot of others.

Bastián thought he looked very acceptable himself in the princely robes. It reminded him of how he had first seen Eisuke donned in military attire. He looked noble then but tense. This evening, he was relaxed.

"Is this too bold?" Bastián asked. "You and me?"

Eisuke shook his head. "Having a servant with me is expected. Same rules as before, I'm afraid, but having you at my side will make it one of the better celebrations I've had in some time."

Bastián hoped it would be. The prince deserved to enjoy his country's festivities instead of hiding away like a horrific creature.

They walked there in silence with Eisuke giving a friendly nod to the other people they passed on their way to the grounds. Bastián spotted a glow from a hilltop and correctly assumed it was their destination. He could hear the music even from their distance. As they ascended the hill, the smell of grilled and fried foods wafted towards them. He kept the prince in his periphery as his attention was stolen by the intricately crafted lanterns that lined their path and the excitement of each new stall that they passed. No one addressed Eisuke, but his elaborate clothing caused many of the merchants to try selling to him.

"They don't recognize you as a prince, do they?" Bastián asked.

"No," Eisuke said, smiling and waving off an eager merchant. "I don't expect them to. I'm sure my brothers are around here somewhere. They're the ones everyone recognizes."

"How dangerous then, truly, is it for me to be out with you?"

"I'm afraid there is still a threat. It would only take one person to notice me and spread word. I'm certain there are a few already planning to sell the story of an unidentified noble gracing the festival."

"If it makes you feel protected, I'll keep silent."

"Just a little longer," Eisuke said. "I promise."

Despite his words, Eisuke struggled to remain stoic throughout the night. He'd pick out a unique snack from the street vendors for Bastián to eat or ask him to try on a festive garment. Bastián thought he looked as excited as a child would.

He really must not be able to enjoy such celebrations often, Bastián thought.

They visited nearly every food vendor with Eisuke ordering from each one. Soon Bastián had a plate stacked with fried tofu, various steamed buns, and topped off with a takoyaki ball.

"You need to stop giving me food," Bastián said with a laugh. "I can't keep up. And you've hardly had any."

"Oh, I'm allergic to soybeans," Eisuke said. "Don't know why I thought you'd know that. I guess I was living through you."

"How about we go to the stalls that have food you can eat?" Bastián said in a light-hearted way. "Tonight is for you."

Eisuke tried to hide another blush. Something caught his eye, and he excitedly dragged Bastián to a vendor selling festival masks of all kinds of yokai. He hovered his hand over them, settled on one of a cat's face, and gave it to Bastián.

"For you," Eisuke said, smiling.

Bastián took it and placed it askew on his head. "Why did you choose a cat?"

"A nekomata," he corrected. "More vicious and cunning than the bakeneko. Two tails instead of one. Treat the cat well, and it will not come to seek revenge once it transforms into a nekomata. Domestic at first, but wild at heart." He lightly touched his shoulder. "Now, choose one for me."

Bastián went for the obvious. He chose the bright red oni mask painted with wrinkled features and big eyes.

Eisuke frowned. "Not sure if I should be insulted by this or not."

"It's a good thing," Bastián said. "Terrifying at first, but then you understand the outward appearance is only meant to protect what's held dear."

"I'll take that," he said, bending so Bastián could affix the mask to his head.

They continue to enjoy the festival long into the night. Bastián found himself keeping a careful eye on Eisuke. He caught him by the arm twice as he stumbled over a loose stone.

"Maybe we should return to the palace."

Eisuke shook his head. "We haven't seen the best part yet."

Bastián smiled weakly and agreed. He was unconvinced the prince wasn't close to overexertion, but Bastián trusted his judgment. He followed Eisuke to a throng of people crowded at the top of the hill. After assessing the crowd, Eisuke led him back down to the lake shore. They settled on a small patch of fresh grass overlooking the lake. Right now, there wasn't much to see except the dull illuminations from the lanterns on the black water.

Alcohol had loosened his tongue, and Eisuke talked at length about everything from the festival's history to local legends about the flora and fauna. Some sounded more like whimsical ghost stories rather than anything his hunter training would treat as fact. Still, Eisuke seemed to be enjoying telling them, and Bastián listened attentively regardless.

They ate the last of the food they had gotten at the vendors. The dishes were nearly cold, but still they were delicious. Bastián held a sticky rice ball up to Eisuke's mouth.

"Should we be doing that?" the prince asked.

Bastián smiled. "Isn't it normal for a servant to feed his master?"

It wasn't. At least not in the way Bastián delicately put the dessert to the prince's lips and let his fingers linger on his chin. Or in the way his thumb wiped a bit of syrup from the corner of his mouth.

A bang and flash of light startled Bastián, alerting his hunter instincts. Eisuke, however, pointed across the water and told him to look. They watched as fireworks lit the night sky. Despite his initial resentment, Bastián marveled at this land's beauty. He felt Eisuke grasp his hand. He looked up to meet the smallest smile the prince could afford. Bastián gave him one of his own and squeezed back.

Eisuke leaned next to his ear. "I know a better place to watch these. Would you like to go there with me?"

"Yes, please," Bastián said, exhaling his held breath.

Eisuke led him back to the palace. Once in the semi-privacy of his garden, Eisuke took his hand, betraying his own rules, and quickly brought him to his room, resisting the urge to break into a run. *A good thing,* thought Bastián. He'd likely get too tired if he did, and Bastián certainly wanted him to have energy for whatever the rest of the night brought.

Eisuke slid the door closed and stepped to the open balcony. Bastián reflexively looked for the moon, but it was a dark night, and the sky was obscured by clouds. He trusted his record keeping, but seeing the lunar phase would have reassured him that he was right.

"The show is that way," Eisuke said.

He pointed opposite the direction Bastián was facing. Bastián awkwardly laughed off his faux pas and turned toward the fireworks. Bastián wouldn't consider this a better view but knew that hadn't been the true intent behind Eisuke's words. He found himself watching the prince more than the show. Eisuke rested his folded arms on the railing, and his gaze was transfixed by the show. Bastián admired his soft smile and the way the wind lightly lifted the loose fabric of his robes and the ends of his hair.

Loud explosions made Bastián look back to the sky. He watched the climax of the show and strongly felt he needed his own release. Bastián turned Eisuke's head toward his own and kissed him. Eisuke gripped the railing, steadying himself against the eagerness of Bastián's mouth.

"I thought you promised to keep me from using too much energy."

"That was only while we were at the festival," Bastián said. He leaned up to him again and put his arms around his neck. "That doesn't apply to what we choose to do after."

Eisuke gently removed Bastián's arms and closed his eyes. Bastián was confused until he noticed his deep breaths and slight shake of his hands. Eisuke was trying to build up courage. The prince opened his eyes, took Bastián's hand, and shifted his pupils to his bed mat. Bastián nodded.

At first, they only continued the kiss. When Eisuke reached for Bastián's robe, he quickly clutched the cloth together. Now, Bastián was nervous, squeezing the prince's hand so hard he was surprised Eisuke didn't say anything.

"Eisuke," he said shakily. "I have to tell you something first."

"It's okay," Eisuke said in a calm voice. "I already know."

"You…know?"

"Aito bathed and dressed you. Of course, I know. Why do you think I was so willing to give you back potentially dangerous talismans? I knew there was something you needed."

"So, you don't care that…that…"

"Your spirit was born inside the wrong body?" Eisuke smiled. "We have far stranger things happen here than that. Furniture becoming sentient, ghost whales patrolling the sea, catfish causing earthquakes—"

"Is that what you view me as? Another oddity for your records?"

Eisuke shook his head. "No, I don't. Those may not have been the best examples to use." He stumbled over his words. "You're hardly anything strange. Not to me. I can't say everyone here would think the same. I—I want to acknowledge your fear, but you needn't have it here with me. The guards painted you as a deceitful witch I needed protection from. But I know you're not that. We're both human no matter our differences."

No, we're not.

"I don't usually face compassion in these circumstances." Bastián grew pensive and took a long pause. "I don't worry about the things people may call me. I feared I'd be killed outright when I was told to undress before your guard. My father always cautioned me to not let it be known unless necessary. Maybe there were others back in my homeland who wouldn't react so violently. Maybe with my mother's tribe. She, too, viewed the spirit superior to the body. But I had to grow up in the guild instead. With them, the risk for me was always death."

"Why would you take that risk with me? I don't want you to be afraid."

Because you don't know what you are. "Because of that. I'm not afraid of you. You could have had me killed several times over, but you didn't. Maybe that's an awfully low set of expectations. I shouldn't forgive you for what you did to me and my crew. But I believe the kindness you've shown me to be genuine."

Eisuke touched the ends of his robe. "May I show you more of that kindness?"

Bastián nodded and lay back, letting the prince shift his weight on top of him. With Eisuke's help, he discarded the rest of his clothing. Eisuke's eyes traveled across his body with an approving gaze. The scarring on his chest was faint, but Bastián always thought it must look apparent to a partner. Eisuke lightly touched the scars, and Bastián confirmed with a nod what used to be there.

"What would you like me to do?"

Bastián guided his hand to his enlarged clitoris. "Two fingers, back and forth."

He demonstrated briefly and Eisuke followed, motioning his fingers like they were around a small penis. Bastián's pelvis bucked in his hand.

"Does it feel that good?" Eisuke asked.

"Yes, but you're also poking against me a lot. Driving me a bit wild wishing you were poking *into* me instead."

Eisuke's face reddened, and Bastián thought it cute. They kissed, and Bastián slipped the elegant kimono over his thin shoulders. It was true Bastián didn't find the prince's body very attractive, supernaturally starved as it was, but he was increasingly finding that not to matter.

"I hope this isn't offensive to ask," Eisuke said, "but is there a concern that I could—" He lightly poked below Bastián's navel. He felt too embarrassed asking directly.

Confused for a moment, Bastián hazarded a guess. "Get me pregnant?"

"Yeah, that. Not exactly been a worry before."

Bastián shook his head. "I don't have a uterus." He flattened Eisuke's hand over a faint scar. He might never have noticed it if Bastián didn't point it out. "I know some very useful body-mending spells."

"I'll have to get you your magic talisman back. You sound like a powerful magician."

Eisuke didn't move his hand, nor did Bastián lift his. The scar was at the top of his pelvic region. He held the prince's gaze. This alone felt intimate. Bastián had dared to let Eisuke in on his truth, and he had accepted it.

Bastián guided Eisuke's head down for a kiss. This broke the prince's stillness.

"Tell me what you need me to do," Eisuke said, stopping the kiss. "I want you to be comfortable."

Bastián smiled gratefully. "I don't have much experience myself. It's difficult to get that when exposing yourself to your partner risks anything from ridicule to death."

"I won't put you through that," Eisuke said, moving his hand down to Bastián's hip. "You don't have to have that fear with me."

"Being who I am doesn't grant me the luxury to ignore that fear." He touched the side of Eisuke's face, tucking the stray hairs behind his ear. "But trust me that living as something I'm not would be far worse."

Bastián guided him into another kiss before he had the opportunity to speak more platitudes. He did appreciate the acceptance more than he could voice. Eisuke accepted and respected him. That was all he needed him to do. Too often the words of others ended up sounding empty and pitying.

Bastián told Eisuke how to pleasure him. He told him when he did it wrong. He certainly made it known when he did it right.

Eisuke massaged oil along his inner thighs until he reached his hole and slipped a finger in. Bastián turned his head and stuffed a pillow in his mouth, muffling his pleasurable grunts and moans.

After adding another finger and a light massage of his inner channel, Eisuke removed his hand from his aroused partner. He leaned over and kissed him, holding his hard penis in one hand with the other pressing gently on Bastián's knee. He entered and let out a loud grunt as if expelling an hour's worth of held breath. He dropped to his elbows and breathed against Bastián's shoulder.

"Are you okay?" Bastián asked.

"Yeah," Eisuke said, perching back up. "It's just been a while, and by the gods you feel nice."

"You feel really good, too," he said, encouraging him with a kiss. "But I think you can make me feel even better."

He knew Eisuke wasn't aggressive, and nothing felt smoother than this monster inserting himself inside him. He cared about his pleasure, and Bastián believed the prince cared about him.

He also remembered his admittance that he wasn't very experienced. Neither was Bastián, but he knew how to get himself off. Eisuke was slower than Bastián had imagined sex would be, but he had sufficiently stimulated him before putting his penis in. All Bastián needed was for him to be slow and rhythmic.

Bastián pushed aside all his doubt as a hunter. He relaxed in his lover's rhythm. Eisuke's breaths became increasingly labored. Bastián squeezed tightly around him, angling his clitoris so that it was extra stimulated with each of his thrusts. He wasn't going to force the prince to exhaustion, but wanted to chase his own orgasm, too. Eisuke's short nails dug into his back, and Bastián's pelvic muscles shuddered around him. Caught off guard by the feeling of his partner's orgasm, Eisuke reached his with a surprised groan. Bastián truly felt wonderful as the prince came into him. He lazily looked up at Eisuke, saw his stance wobble, and Bastián quickly grabbed either side of his arms, steadying him.

"I have you," Bastián said.

"Thanks," Eisuke said, trying to ease his breath.

Bastián gently helped roll him to the side and onto his back.

"See? I told you about the overexertion."

"Is this my fault, then?" Bastián asked, caressing his arm.

"No." He took his hand and kissed it. "Maybe a little."

"Next time, I'll be on top," he said with a playful smile.

"Good," he said, laughing and pulling his head close to him. "I think I'd like that."

"I like hearing you laugh," Bastián replied after a kiss to his chest.

Eisuke stroked his hair with a soft smile. "I'm going to fall asleep soon," he said. "You can stay. Sleep here for the night. With me."

"That sounds lovely."

Bastián rested his head on his rising and falling chest. His hunter instinct screamed at him again. He was a demon. He killed or enslaved all his companions. He'd enslaved him. But no sense of anger or revenge could cross his mind. Instead, he shifted slightly, getting more comfortable next to his partner. He stroked the side of his head, careful to caress the slight ridge on his skull. The only revenge he wanted to chase was for Eisuke. He had been kept weak and ignorant. Eisuke had no idea why he was treated the way he was, and he deserved that knowledge.

CHAPTER 12

Two days left before the full moon. Bastián had to get his necklace back. He felt an aching in his bones as it neared time for them to pop, twist, and contort. Luckily, he didn't think Eisuke would hesitate to give him anything from his personal belongings.

They met at their usual spot in the garden although the weather was quickly turning too cold for it to be comfortable. It helped that Eisuke had taken to sitting very close to him. Bastián wondered how his frail body could handle the chill without so much as a shiver, but he supposed he could thank his yokai blood for that.

"I have something important to ask you," Bastián said. "I need—"

Eisuke held up a hand. "Of course but let me give you something first."

Surprised, Bastián agreed and watched Eisuke take out a small package from his robe wrapped in thin paper. He handed it to Bastián.

"A gift?" he asked, turning it over in his hands. He felt a calmness wash over him as he handled the package.

"More of a return," Eisuke said.

With a skeptical gaze at the prince, Bastián unwrapped the package. A chunky chain with a canine-like pendant fell into his hands. He didn't know how to react. This was the exact thing he tried to ask him for. He popped the locket open, confirming the wolfsbane was still in there. He smelled it. The oils hadn't gone bad yet either.

"I don't—why this?" Bastián asked.

"You need it, don't you?"

"Yes, but…you shouldn't know that I do."

"I had some reading material of my own," Eisuke said with a coy smile, "though it was hard to decipher at points. You should work on your handwriting."

"My journal," Bastián concluded, still flabbergasted that Eisuke knew. "I forgot that information was in there."

Bastián had used his journal to track the moon phases and any symptoms he experienced leading up to a full moon. But he had entered that data into it years ago. He had forgotten it was the same one he used to record his recent hunts.

Bastián looked sadly at the pendant. "Nothing about me was ever secret to you, was it?"

"That's not true," Eisuke said. "Yes, I knew your secrets since we first sat together in this garden. But I knew what you kept hidden not what you shared with others. And you, a were-creature, bearing your guild's crest and coming across an ocean to hunt a demonic spirit—I might as well have known nothing for how little sense that makes."

Bastián remained fixated as if he hadn't heard his words. "You said you've read our texts. Did you read any bestiaries?"

He nodded.

"Then you've read about werewolves."

"I have, but the beast you kept drawing didn't look like any wolf."

"I'm not," he said. He held the pendant up to Eisuke. "When you look at this do you see a wolf or a cat?"

Eisuke tilted his head. "It's rather hard to tell. The style is very geometric."

"The ambiguity is intentional. My body follows the typical werewolf cycle, but I appear more cat-like when I'm in that form."

"There are records solely about the hunt of werewolves written by your guild," Eisuke said. "And you're one of them? How have you hidden from them for so long?"

Bastián put on the necklace the familiar weight of it comforting him. "I haven't. My guild were the ones to do it to me."

"I see. Saints in your world can actually turn sinners into werewolves. What did you do to invoke their wrath?"

"It wasn't me," Bastián said. "It was my father. I told you your records were outdated."

"So…," Eisuke said, "if you didn't have that locket, you'd turn into a huge cat every full moon?"

"Yeah. A huge skeletal, undead abomination that looks like something from a nightmare."

"Was that on purpose?"

Bastián shook his head. "I don't think so. I don't think they have that power. I like to think they don't, at least. My mother was a shapeshifter herself. Several in her tribe were. Her animal form—she was a jaguar. I think something got messed up when they tried to curse me. I hope so, anyway."

"Why hope for that?"

"Because it means I inherited some of her power. And if I inherited that, maybe I inherited some of her control over it. My eyes weren't like this before. Both blue when I was a child. Maybe the yellow is because it never truly goes dormant. Maybe I won't have to forever wear *this*."

"Are you mad that you have to wear it to not transform or mad you can't transform at will?"

"Ha," he said drily. "You can already read me well. I've seen far too much injustice being a hunter. It'd be much easier to subdue either side if I could tear their bones apart without endangering the innocent."

"Do you hate that side of you?"

"I don't. I know I should, but there's something endearing about it. Especially if I can gain control of it."

Eisuke sat in thought. "Your mother…it wasn't your typical colonizers who killed her, was it?"

"The guild did it," Bastián said sharply. "It was a great honor to be able to access one's nagual spirit. It wasn't a curse or something out of their control. The guild didn't see it that way. My father helped hide them. It worked until it didn't."

"I know your guild is violent," Eisuke said, "but did they truly want to annihilate an entire tribe for peacefully existing even if they were beasts?"

"They'd normally be encouraged not to resort to such means, but each side was caught in a back-and-forth retaliation. The guild argues they were wronged first, but I don't believe it. Other tribes report their shapeshifters as cruel beings. I think the guild assumed all were like that and didn't bother to check if it were different. I think they killed one of theirs first. And then my grandfather died by the tribe's hand. That was the incident the guild couldn't forgive. Not the tribe and not my father for trying to help his own family's killers."

"Except the tribe was his family, too. With your mother."

"Exactly," Bastián said. "He had come to realize how wrong the guild was about things. He'd rather lose his awful father than his wife and child. Which the guild knew. So, they took both from him."

"Tried to," Eisuke corrected.

Bastián thumbed the locket. "I don't know. Maybe they did. I still don't know why he sent me out here. You were right. It only makes sense if it were a suicide mission."

"I said that because I had incorrectly assumed your relationship with your father was poor. I hadn't realized the love he has for you."

"He didn't know what to do with me, not at first," Bastián said. "I was only eleven when it happened. I remember the first time I turned. An awful, excruciating pain in my limbs and spine. I ran to him crying. He had fought enough werewolves to recognize what was happening. I didn't, though. I didn't understand it at all. Nor why he brought me to the cellar and chained me to the floor."

Eisuke crept his hand to be on top of Bastián's. The coolness of the prince's palm startled him out of the pained memory.

"It, um." Bastián stumbled on his words. "It happened twice more before he left the chains off. Then four more moons before he had crafted this necklace. There were a few failures before he got it right. By then I understood as much as I could at that age. It never stopped hurting to hear that lock turn after he left."

"How bad is it? When you turn. It sounds dire. Or at least that your father treated it that way."

"I don't really know." Bastián tried to force a smile, but it didn't stick. "I haven't turned in over a decade. I feel it wanting to be loosed each full moon—a crawling, itching sensation throughout my body. A bit of chaos that makes it harder to ignore certain physical impulses." He ran his thumb over the grooves on the pendant's face.

Eisuke took a long pause to think. "When you say, 'certain physical impulses….' And this close to a full moon…. Did we—did you—?"

Bastián sighed. He reached out to touch the prince's worried face. "I wanted to have sex with you, and I'm glad we did. It might have made me agree more readily, but even then, it's still me." He tried to laugh and was more successful than his previous attempt at levity. "Honestly, it probably just made me come faster. So, you might have to work a little harder next time."

Eisuke took the hand from his face and let it rest in his own. "As long as I have the energy, I'll work as hard as you need me to." Eisuke looked down to the hand he was holding. He grazed his thumb over the metal band on Bastián's finger. "When I asked if you needed anything, you chose this. You'll turn into an uncontrollable, violent beast without your necklace, but you picked this instead. Why?"

"My reasoning, um, isn't very good. Pretty selfish, actually."

"You have to tell me after saying that."

Bastián took an exhausted breath. "I was your prisoner, and I had several weeks until the next full moon. I thought I could possibly root out whatever evil my mission assigned to this place. If I couldn't, well, it'd make for a hell of an escape attempt when I turned."

Eisuke studied him with pursed lips. Bastián hoped he wasn't too angered by his original intentions. "Right…I'm not going to dwell on that. You didn't tell me what that ring does, only why you didn't choose the necklace."

Bastián held up his hand and splayed his fingers. "I need this more. I don't truly know what would happen without it. Maybe I'm old enough that it wouldn't have much effect if taken away."

"It keeps you being *you*."

"Yes," Bastián said. "That's the best way to describe it. I'm grateful my father became supportive, but he wasn't at first."

"He was dealing with a were-creature already."

"And yet *that* he accepted easier than my masculinity. He did accept it, eventually, but he insisted I go through puberty first. Said I couldn't know how foreign my body felt if it hadn't had a chance to fully develop. Trust me that I didn't need that experience to change anything about how I felt."

"That's why you have the chest scars."

"Yeah. I wish I didn't. Just reminds me of the deep depression I was in as a teenager. It's also awkward to explain why I can't take my shirt off ever. And even after all this time wearing this ring, my voice still cracks, and I can barely grow anything but a mustache."

Eisuke scooted closer to him and lay a hand on his thigh. "Bastián, my voice cracks occasionally. And there's a reason my face is smooth. For your scars—I can't tell you how to feel about them. I know this is something I may never be able to fully understand, not in the way you understand it, but there isn't a single standard you need to adhere to."

Bastián restrained his criticism. Eisuke wasn't the best comparison. Not with his body starved as it was. Not with—Bastián had to stop that type of thinking. Comparing himself to other men was a bad habit of his. He judged them on the same standard he judged himself and no one benefitted.

Bastián protectively held his ringed hand against his chest. "You've accepted everything that I've been told, if shared, would be dangerous. I'm not used to that feeling."

Bastián could tell from Eisuke's silent pensiveness he struggled with what to say. It always felt tiring to explain his personal history. Even if there was no opposition, like with Eisuke, there was always tension that he could be misinterpreted, whether accidentally or maliciously. He tapped the teacup in front of Eisuke, steam still rising from it.

"What about you?" Bastián said automatically.

"Me?"

Bastián didn't look up, hiding his mortified face. He had meant to change the topic, but didn't realize he was going to reflexively reference Eisuke's hidden nature. "Oh. It's—I mean, if you had something like my werecat. What would you think about it?"

"I guess it would depend on what it was." Eisuke tipped the teacup so he could see the leaves at the bottom. "Do you know something I don't?"

"I—I don't know. But, I mean, maybe…"

"Bastián. Tell me."

"I think you're what I was sent to find."

He expected Eisuke to laugh. It's what he had done the first time he mentioned it. Instead, he stared plaintively into the teacup.

"You didn't know your mother," Bastián explained hurriedly. "Your father clearly doesn't want you in the line of succession. And yeah. You've been drinking whatever that is all your life. I don't think your weakness is a coincidence."

"What is it?" he asked sternly. "You examined it. What is in it?"

"I don't have access to all my kits for a proper examination."

"Don't give me that," he said harshly. "You're a hunter, you took some leaves for examination, and said you had a conclusion. Tell me."

"Blood. That's the worst of the smell. Dried blood, for sure. Other bitter herbs that I don't recognize but remind me of what's in this locket."

"If I am…what you say, why would blood make me weak?"

"It's not the type you need. Just what keeps you alive."

"Nonhuman, you mean."

Bastián nodded.

He pressed his fingers against his temples. "I can't believe that readily. And this isn't solid proof. You know that, right?"

"I do, Eisuke, I promise you that." He reached for his hand, but he pulled it away.

"Not now," he said in that same harsh tone. "I need time to think."

"I had to tell you."

"I appreciate that. But telling me this after your own confession?" He shook his head.

"What does that mean?"

"You're biased. What if you believe it because you want me to be like you? What if I am just a simple, frail human? What would I mean to you then?"

"There are ridges on your skull."

"Childhood injury."

"Symmetrically?!"

"There are simpler answers. That's what I'm saying. I—I don't know. I need a moment. I told you that."

"At the shrine," Bastián said, "a kitsune confirmed it all with me. She told me what I could use to glimpse your oni form. When I massaged—"

"Stop!" he said violently. "You enchanted me?! They may be Inari's messengers, but kitsune are not above playing cruel pranks. She could have given you something to create an illusion instead of dispelling one."

"I thought you trusted my hunter instinct."

Eisuke closed his eyes. "You didn't answer me. What if I'm not a monster? Would you still be here?"

Bastián didn't speak. No. He wouldn't. His forgiveness had come because he recognized Eisuke was in a prison of his own. His care for him grew solely because he felt a kinship with his hidden nature.

"I need to be alone," Eisuke said, not waiting for a reply. "I want you to leave."

"Eisuke—"

He held up a hand. "I don't want you pretending to be a servant anymore. I'll give you clearance if you want to stay in Yasunai. Tell my guards where you'll be, and I'll come find you in a few days."

"Promise?"

Eisuke seemed caught off guard by Bastián's sincere tone, as if surprised the hunter would still care for him.

"I promise," Eisuke said.

CHAPTER 13

Bastián found lodging near to the palace. Eisuke had his guard escort him and pay for wherever he chose. Albeit having the Yasunai guard with him forewent any payment.

He felt lost, yet found minimal comfort in his familiar hunter's garb. The guard had begrudgingly given him back his spellcasting talisman and weapons. He had had everything returned, yet it all felt strangely foreign to him.

Two days passed, and Bastián grew restless. After three, he was angry. By five, he turned concerned. It hadn't truly been long. He tried repeating this to himself. But the prince had said a *few* days. He had to trust Eisuke would reach out to him.

He needed money and a distraction. His specialized skills were suited to being a hunter but not much else.

Disgust roiled in his guts reading the local bounty requests. Humans wanted to be rid of creatures that caused little to no harm. He forced himself to accept the ones where he could relocate the creature rather than kill it. Many yokai Bastián encountered on these hunts didn't understand human customs and were obliged to leave once he explained them.

He avoided the bigger bounties. These usually required more violent tactics, and he couldn't bring himself to accept them. One in particular saddened him: a bounty for a witch living at an old temple. A large bounty, too. A hunter could live off it for a year.

Bastián would bet the old crone did nothing but mind her own business, yet humans viewed her as a vile spirit desecrating the land.

After a week, it finally dawned on him: Eisuke's birthday. The kitsune said it was around the same time as the full moon. Therefore—

Shit.

Bastián rushed to the palace. The guards had either had no memory of him or no kindness toward him. As he was about to be escorted away, Aito caught sight of the disturbance and stopped them. Bastián broke free from their slacked grasps and approached Aito.

"I need to see Eisuke," he stated.

"That's not possible," Aito said.

Bastián's brow furrowed. "What do you mean? How is it not possible?!"

"He's not here," the old servant stated through pursed lips. "He was sent away."

"Sent away? I don't understand."

"I think you very much do understand, *hunter.*"

He caught onto the insinuation. "Is he hurt?"

"No, but the emperor has contracted a private bounty for his capture, requested as dead or neutralized. The same hunter proved his worth by killing Eisuke's mother. You see, we no longer have access to the special concoction that kept him safe to be around."

"Concoction?" Bastián asked. "Do you mean the tea? And his mother… I thought… the witch. You had her killed. How could you do that to Eisuke? He relied on you for twenty-five years!"

"I follow the will of the emperor before the well-being of his bastard son," Aito said stoically. "However, if someone happened to have forgotten to lock the cell, and Eisuke escaped, I'd call it all just poor luck."

"When did he leave?"

"Four days ago."

"Four!? The trail's bound to have gone cold!"

"Well, I'd say you and our contract hunter are on even ground now. Might I suggest if you want him back, you use the skills your namesake claims to have, and go hunt." He shrewdly looked to the guards. They did not seem to be paying attention. Aito dropped his voice to a whisper. "Start on a northern path toward the mountains. And hurry."

"Thank you," Bastián said, reading between the lines of the old servant's responses.

Aito waved him on. "Best you leave," he said in his normal tone, eying the uninterested guards. He whispered to him again. "Good luck, hunter."

Bastián nodded then left, wasting no time.

He scoured as close to the palace's northward grounds as he could get. As expected, he found no anomalous foot trail. He cursed himself more than any guard or servant who had allowed this to happen to Eisuke. He was the one to have waited a week before realizing his mistake.

In his haste, he almost missed a promising detail. There was no foot trail, but there was a hoof trail. The spacing of the hoof prints was unusual, as if the animal tenderly put weight on one leg. Lame, probably. Old? Maybe. Perhaps a very old horse too docile to fear an oni. The hoof prints did indeed lead north, and Bastián followed.

Bastián knew he couldn't cover enough ground on foot, but the money he gained through the simple hunts was enough to buy his own horse. Not the fittest or fastest horse, but a sturdy bay gelding that was more of a pony than a steed.

He looked at each new bounty posted in each new village he passed through. The emperor had personally contracted the bounty, but that didn't prevent others from posting about any shadowy creature threatening their peace. Yet he found no clues.

Worse, the hoof trail stopped. He felt ridiculous asking the villagers about an elderly horse, but he did so until one of them pointed him towards a small feral herd. Bastián then felt even more stupid trying to distinguish one horse from a herd of brown, dark brown, and *look there!*, a light brown. He couldn't remember the color of Eisuke's horse. It was not a detail he would have thought he should commit to memory the day he was captured. He did see at least two that looked like they had lost their topline weight with age. Even then all that it confirmed was that Eisuke let his horse go before it perished from exhaustion.

Bastián retread his search route, but anything else that could have helped was gone. He felt crushed and hopeless, but he refused to give up. So many people treated inhuman creatures as evil. Bastián had seen it enough in his time as a hunter. He had made a secret promise he would protect the prince. The despair that he had failed tore at his heart.

He clutched his necklace, wishing he had that control he longed for. Another full moon had come, and, if he could release it, he could possibly pick up on a trail his human senses couldn't. But he didn't trust his beast would understand this, or any, command he tried to give it before the moon rose high in the night sky.

It began raining one night. The weather was quickly turning cold. This was likely the last rain before it changed to snow. If Eisuke was out there, all trace would be washed away now.

He watched the flashes of lightning. He should hate the cleansing of the earth it brought. Instead, seeing something as angry as he felt brought him comfort.

Another flash. This time he saw something red illuminated in the sky. That couldn't be. It must just be the after image of the bright light. But there it was again in the next one.

Bastián ran out into the storm, rain pelting his face. He shielded his eyes and hoped he wasn't acting as a lightning rod.

He saw it even without the flashes of lightning. Faint, but there. A red line weaving its way through the trees and up into the sky.

Follow the red thread.

That's what the monk at the first temple had told him. Should he ever despair, follow it. Bastián was incredulous. Were the spirits of this land reaching out to him?

He rushed to follow it, anxiously settling his lodging tab. He gave the host two minutes before he slammed enough coin to be twice or triple—he did not check that closely—what he owed. He mounted his horse, and rode off, following the red thread and feeling like a madman. His hunter rationale made him question it more than once, but hallucination was the strongest lead he had right now.

CHAPTER 14

The thread stopped at a rural village tucked between the mountains. Bastián was frustrated it couldn't pinpoint Eisuke's exact location, but he was confident this was the right area. Or, at least, he repeated that confidence to himself as he began reconnaissance.

He listened to the villagers when he visited the local izakaya and food stands. He heard their hushed whispers, their loud complaints, and their fear of an unknown predator. None gave him the details he needed to start tracking, but it assured him he was in the right area. Time to ask directly.

Bastián entered the izakaya on a slow afternoon. The few patrons either treated him to a short glare or tried to avoid looking at him at all. He ordered a drink and leaned on the bar. The owner served him the sharpest look out of all who were there. Feeling unwelcome, Bastián got straight to the point with his questioning.

"Have there been any unusual incidents around here?"

The owner kept his shrewd glare. "Why does that interest you?"

"I'm a hunter," Bastián explained. "Whatever it is, I can track it down and relieve your town of its hunger."

"Are you looking for a bounty?" the owner asked gruffly. "We don't have the kind of money to pay for an extermination."

"It's not—I don't need money for this. It's a personal hunt."

The owner huffed, unamused. "You think that makes you any better? I rather avoid having to clean up the mess your kind leaves."

Bastián was used to some scrutiny when he interacted with locals, but the tavern owner's replies were curt even with that in mind.

"What messes?" Bastián asked.

"We had another one of you here last month. Same thing. Trying to find something that didn't exist. Poisoned and ensnared half the forest trying to root something out."

Bastián grimaced. "I promise you that will not be my method."

"I doubt that," he said. "The other one looked just like you. Wore the exact same getup. Told the exact same promises."

"And he looked *just* like me?"

"A little taller. A little lighter."

"A tall, light-skinned man wearing the same style as me," Bastián stated bluntly. "Anything else you can tell me about him?"

The owner shrugged. "You all look the same to me."

It sounded like someone from his guild, but Bastián thought that was impossible. Although Aito hadn't specified before he sent him off. Only that a hunter had been hired privately. He would have guessed the emperor would have had his own exorcists to call on.

"Did this hunter tell you his name?"

"Nope. Didn't seem to give a damn about any of us. Treated us as if we weren't worth knowing."

Bastián's heartbeat quickened. He had the sudden thought that maybe one of the superior guild members made their way over, suspecting Bastián's crew had failed. If that had happened, Eisuke was in more danger than he'd realized. Bastián could take on any of his peers, but he couldn't match a superior of the guild.

"You said whatever he was hunting didn't exist. Are you certain?"

The owner shrugged again. "We had some livestock attacks a few weeks back. Local patrons here called it anything from a malnourished bear to a white-haired devil. Whatever it was, it hasn't attacked since. Maybe that hunter did catch it after all."

Bastián's throat tightened. He almost forgot to breathe. That wasn't the type of clue he had hoped to find.

"This other hunter. Can you show me where he laid the traps?"

"Don't need to. Go out to the edge of town where the forest meets the last of the pastures. Then just go straight in. That's what he did."

"Thank you," Bastián said. He put extra tip money on the counter. Maybe he could restore a sliver of goodwill from the townspeople.

Much as it had been when he tried to pick up a trail from the palace, most reliable tracks were lost to the weather. He examined the outer perimeter regardless, finding a tuft of white hair stuck on the low-hanging branch of a tree. He frowned as he investigated it. It felt like human hair: long and slightly coarse. Bastián was uncertain what, if any, transformation Eisuke would have gone through, but this hair, opposite to the black Bastián knew him to have, made him uneasy. What if he couldn't recognize the prince anymore?

He remembered the vision that appeared when he had massaged him. Eisuke had white hair then. Holding the memory, he thought of how fine Eisuke's hair was and how often Bastián had yearned to tuck the unruly wisps behind his ear. He could imagine doing the same with this white clump, and his doubts vanished. He would know his prince. He was sure of it.

There wasn't much of a trail to follow, and Bastián had to go off conjecture more often than he preferred. Soon he spotted a rabbit carcass with its neck obliterated. Something had torn and chewed it apart. The kill had to be at least a week old, if not more. The cold preserved the carcass, but fresh snow obscured any blood trail.

Bastián hated tracking in snow. Whether deep or melting, it warped the size and shape of tracks. This frustration gnawed away at his patience, and he was almost ready to end the search for the day when he caught sight of a strange trail in the muddy ground.

It looked as if a significantly sized creature had been dragged. Or had crawled. He observed impressions that were too irregular to be footprints but could be handprints. The damned snow didn't help him draw any conclusion. Still enough remained visible for Bastián to track it.

The trail ended at the ruins of an old home. He could see a mound of something inside the dilapidated exterior. From his distance, it could have been just snow. Bastián stepped forward to investigate, stopping once to observe another rabbit with a ripped apart throat. As he stood, he realized it wasn't snow ahead of him. It was a body with pale gray skin, lying face down. The long white hair blended seamlessly with the snow.

Bastián didn't believe the other hunter could have missed this. His only guess was the previous hunter had gotten impatient and given up. Whatever it was, perhaps the gods' blessing the monk and the kitsune had given him hadn't yet worn off.

With a trembling hand, Bastián pushed on the cold, stiff body. No reaction. He pushed harder, rolling the body onto its back. Bastián retched at the sight but kept himself from vomiting. Yet more powerful than the nausea was the fear he had been too late.

The form that lay before him had two short horns and fine wisps of white hair on its head. The rest of its body was a gray, shriveled husk. Its mouth gaped open into a black maw, and its eyes were an equally soulless void.

Bastián tentatively touched the thing. It might not be Eisuke. He hoped it wasn't. He hoped it was another demon, emaciated and starved. He couldn't tell, and he hated himself for that. He didn't know the beings of this realm as well as he knew the ones of his homeland. He would need help.

He sealed the area around the derelict building and sought the nearest shrine. He prayed at the altar. Told the spirits his predicament. Pleaded for their aid. He left offerings of incense and sake, fruit and flowers, even jewelry he had picked up over the years. Anything that would convince an entity to help him.

No spirits responded to him that night. Nor had he expected them to. But as he prepared to settle in for the next night, he caught the darting of a fox from the corner of his eye. The vulpine could easily be a coincidence, but he set out a choice cut of rabbit anyway. He could use all the grace he could get.

The next night the fox returned. Again, he gave it fresh meat. The third night, the fox patiently waited for him, perched elegantly outside his home. Each night Bastián made an offering to the strangely stoic fox, and each day his composure threatened to break. How had the spirits been so helpful but now tested his patience? If this corpse wasn't Eisuke, he needed to know so he could continue his search. If it was—if it was, he needed to know.

On the fifth night, he was met not by a fox, but a fox-tailed woman. She greeted him with a polite bow. Bastián dropped to his knee in front of the kitsune, more out of a need to hide his frustration rather than show reverence.

"My lady," he said.

The kitsune put a hand over her mouth to hide a laugh. "You needn't be so formal, little hunter. The high priestess sent me to judge the sincerity of your prayers. You pray for a yokai, yes? The kitsune have a tenuous relationship with onis. I'm uncertain how much help we can be."

Bastián did not rise. "The only help I need is with identification. I've found what I believe is the corpse of an oni. I need help identifying its human form."

"How intriguing. Take me to this body."

Bastián led the kitsune to the abandoned home. He removed the seals, both physical and magical. The kitsune spotted the body and knelt next to it.

"Your first issue, dear hunter," she said, "is that this is not a corpse."

Bastián looked at her in shock. She laughed.

"We yokai are spiritual entities. Our physical body can withstand the extremes of deprivation. That being said, this poor boy is nearly past that even for us."

"How—how do I know if it's him?"

"Hm," she hummed, studying the figure. "I cannot sense his appearance, but I can sense his aspect." She closed her eyes. "Oh. Oh, no, that can't be right."

"What is it?"

"You didn't tell us he was royalty." She gazed up at him only to be met with his blank countenance. "Are you still with me, hunter?"

Bastián forced himself back to awareness. "Are you sure? I can't be wrong about this."

"I think the better question is if *you* are sure. You wouldn't protect any old, presumed corpse, would you?"

Bastián didn't know the answer. He had saved common yokai from a hunter's blade but had ignored the big game hunts. If confronted by a powerful creature, surely, he wouldn't strike first. Not now. Not after meeting Eisuke.

"You said he's not dead?" Bastián asked.

She nodded. "Very close, however."

"How do I help him?"

The kitsune studied him with amusement. "Your first question wasn't if this fate of his is reversible. Would you want to save him if he never could regain his human-like form?"

"He doesn't deserve to die like this."

"That's not quite my question, but I'll accept it. Do you know what type of essence he needs?"

"I know he needs blood. Rooster blood sustained him before."

"Animal blood will not suffice this time. He needs human. Or mostly human, in your case."

"Why now? Because he transformed?"

"In part," she agreed. "But his condition is worse than it appears. He was victim to a hunter's trap. No matter how many infected animals he consumed, their blood would not satiate him."

"Which would push him to consume human blood."

The kitsune nodded. "I expect the hunter wanted to drive him into a hunger-filled rage and savage a villager or two, but the former prince refused to break his principle, starving himself instead. Truly a ruthless and cruel way to hunt."

Bastián thought about that tactic, and he tightened a fist. "It sounds like my guild, but none of them should be around."

"You were spared, weren't you? Is it hard to believe another may have been, too?"

Bastián suddenly felt numb. He hadn't thought it possible to be any of his former crew. "Endangering humans to draw out a monster that wouldn't harm them—I can't forgive those tactics."

"Don't," she encouraged, "but for now, the other hunter is not your concern. This oni is." She pointed to his gaping mouth. "Feed him your blood twice daily. After he gains strength, you can incorporate solid foods. He survives off blood, but his physical body will thank you. Still, I must warn he may not recover. Not as you once knew him. Once a yokai loses their connection to humans, they have no need to appear as one. They truly belong to the spirits then."

"I have to try. I owe that to him. I could have helped him more if I found him sooner."

The kitsune nodded her understanding and helped Bastián move the body. As she departed, she told him to return to the shrine if he needed further assistance.

Bastián swaddled the husk and laid it near the fire. He cut along his palm. He squeezed his fingers together and held them over that black hole mouth. The jaws shuddered at the taste of blood, attempting to close around the sweet liquid but unable to do so. It took all Bastián's will to suppress the instinct to shrink back from the sight. This was Eisuke—maybe—and even if it wasn't him, he wouldn't let it die. It was a victim of his guild's cruel methods. Watching those traces of life, Bastián knew the answer to the kitsune's question that he had avoided. He wasn't a monster hunter anymore.

He continued the twice daily feeding with minimal improvement. The oni's talons grew sharp, and his hair thickened, so Bastián knew his blood was helping. But still, the body would do little more than moan and tremble with those blank eyes staring right through him.

As Bastián finished the most recent feeding, he felt hopelessness sink in. Maybe he had been too late. A loud growling made him turn back to the bed, hand on his sword hilt.

The body was gone.

Shit. He swiftly turned on his heels to see nothing behind him. He turned back and right into the waiting talons of a starving oni.

His hunter training told him to go for his sword. Swing an arc in front of him and end this demented creature. He didn't. He held up crossed arms, blocking the clawing and snapping demon. Bastián could see no recognition in those eyes. Glaringly red and filled with only the urge to devour.

"Eisuke!" he tried to beg. "Stop!"

Instead of pausing his assault, the oni fought harder as if incensed by the plea. His sharpened nails aimed for the side of Bastián's neck, but he moved just in time for them to miss, his shoulder taking the blow instead. The talons easily sliced through both fabric and skin. Bastián used all his energy for one last shove, pushing the oni off him.

"Eisuke, please," he begged again, "remember me. And if you can't, consume me. I'd rather you took my life to survive than I kill you."

It was no use. Even this didn't stir anything human in the demon's countenance. His partner was gone, consumed by the monster within him.

Bastián dropped his hands.

If Eisuke was gone, he had nothing left. No crew and no guild to return to. He couldn't kill the former prince.

The demon descended on him. He knocked Bastián to the ground. Even though Bastián had seen no teeth in that gaping maw, he felt sharp fangs pierce his skin. The last he saw was the red-black eyes of his demon.

CHAPTER 15

Bastián was surprised when he woke. His neck felt terribly sore, and his legs trembled as he tried to stand. He knew he had lost a lot of blood. He assumed the beast who once was his partner had fled. Yet as he scoured the room, he saw the covers lumped up. He should use his little strength to fetch food or water, but an incessant pull toward the creature made him check first.

If he had had any excess fluid in his system, he would have cried with happiness.

Eisuke's body appeared waif-like and malnourished, but Bastián could tell it was him. For the first time since picking him up from the snow, he could discern the features of the former prince. He wanted to give him more blood, but this time he listened to his own body and stumbled to the stove pot for some broth.

He drank the salty, meaty liquid. He made a mental note to return to the shrine and thank the kitsune for their help. He poured the broth into a bowl for Eisuke. He held his hand over it. It looked so pale. He wasn't well enough to feed his own blood. He took a butcher cut of pork, pressed down on it, and poured the collected blood into the bowl. This would have to do until Bastián recovered.

While he no longer had a gaping hole in his face, Eisuke still appeared unconscious. Bastián carefully spooned the soup into his mouth, checking his throat to be sure he reflexively swallowed it.

He often went to the shrine, feeding the foxes that called it home. The kitsune wasn't always there. Not in her human form. Bastián supposed any of the foxes could be her, especially if the fox was emboldened by his presence instead of cautious. Once a fox followed him home. He let her into the house, and she transformed, stretching her limbs and dusting off her tail. She raised her face up, smelling the meaty soup simmering over the fire.

"If you're looking for advice on an offering," she said. "You could do worse than a bowl of whatever is emitting this wonderful aroma."

"It might be better going to you instead of…." Bastián said with a sigh. "It's not going well with Eisuke. It's been a week, and I can't see any progress."

"You mean, it's *only* been a week," she said with her effervescent amusement. "I expected you to know this will take time, silly hunter."

Bastián did not appreciate how flippantly she spoke.

"I haven't yet seen any recognition from him."

The fox woman walked to the form on the bed. Bastián watched as she gently opened each eye with her slender fingers. To Bastián, all he saw was chaos in those red and black eyes.

"He's not far from recovery," she said. "He is between realms, yes, but that he has regained a more human-like form is very promising. It shows he does not wish to stay as the monster you found him as." She chuckled. "But certainly, you know it's not all bad to be a monster once in a while."

Bastián frowned at the implication. "If he needs human blood, why would mine help him? Did it inadvertently hurt him more? Should I—I can't kill for him."

"Calm down, little hunter," she said. "You are human enough that it sustains him. In fact, it is an ideal time to start again, isn't it? The moon energizes you, and he will taste that energy in the blood."

Energizes. Aggravates. Bastián supposed one was similar enough to the other.

"Did you know he would attack me?" he asked.

"Know is such a strong word. Even if he didn't, I knew he'd get enough of your blood regardless. You'd have grown distraught and fed him more than I said."

"If you knew that was the way to restore him, why didn't you tell me?"

"I respect my fellow yokai," she said, "but it's wise not to let them gorge on whatever it is that sustains them. Especially one that had been intentionally starved. That's when they lose control over their urge to feed and become a problem to the humans. If he could be revived with the rationed blood, it had to be tried first."

"That doesn't tell me why I couldn't have known."

"I suppose you could have, but they binge. It is not their fault. Sometimes being opportunistic feeders means they become greedy when they finally get a meal. Other times, they simply do not have control. But your little oni is lucky."

"How so?"

"He has been fed tiny amounts of blood all his life. He has not been conditioned to devour humans any time he gets the chance."

"Is the toxin gone, then? Can he take in animal blood if needed?"

"I do believe your blood flushed it from his system. But remember, that is not the ideal sustenance for him. Animal blood permits him to live. It does not give him strength. Yokai have sustained themselves for years with only one prime kill. Some much, much longer. He may only need a few sips a week. Especially from someone like you, the hunter who is animal and human both."

"I understand," he said and gave a slight bow. "Thank you for your guidance."

"I was serious about the offering," she said behind a giggle. She stuck a finger in the pot, unaffected by the heat, and licked the broth from her hand. "Bring this next time you pray. Our fox friends would enjoy a warm meal on these cold days."

With a promise from Bastián, she left. Bastián turned to the lump of gray on the bed, knife in hand. Another time in another life, he would be preparing to stab that knife through the monster's heart. Instead, he held the blade to his own skin, cutting his lower forearm. He positioned it over that mouth full of dagger-like teeth. The jaws instinctively pulled his arm closer, sucking in the air from between them and suctioning his lips to Bastián's skin.

Bastián slipped into a meditative state. His focus was only on the feeling of blood being siphoned from his arm. He was so deep into this state that when the feeling stopped, he was confused by its absence rather than relieved. He forced himself out of the reverie.

Eisuke's head slumped back to the pillow. Bastián, feeling a bit of vertigo from the blood loss, got onto the bed with his partner. He held Eisuke's thin body against him as he slept. He needed to feel his breathing. Remember he was still in there. Despite the fear. Despite the danger.

After a few nights, the prince spoke.

"Bastián," he muttered.

"Eisuke!" he said, turning his sallow face toward him.

He didn't say anything more, but the hand across his arm tightened ever so slightly. Bastián pressed his forehead against his shoulder.

"I'm here, Eisuke. Please. I'm here."

Two days later, Bastián caught sight of red pupil eyes set against black. Eyes that looked back at him with recognition.

"Bastián, am I…?"

"Alive," Bastián said, embracing him. "You're alive."

"How?"

He wouldn't get an answer as Bastián held onto him and cried.

"It's okay," Eisuke said. "I think."

"I'm sorry," Bastián said, sucking down a deep breath. "I didn't expect to do that. I just—I didn't know if I'd ever speak to you again."

"How long has it been?"

"Just over a month."

"A month!?"

"At least the worst of winter is nearly over," Bastián offered.

He brought up a thin arm. "No wonder I look like this."

"You—you were a lot worse when I found you."

Eisuke noticed the heaviness in his tone. "Did I do something to you?"

Bastián shook his head. "No. Nothing that wouldn't have been expected."

"I did, didn't I? Bastián, I—"

He touched his cheek. "I know. I don't blame you, and I'm still here. That's all that matters." He glanced at the pot over the fire. "Let me boil more water now that you're awake."

Eisuke nodded though he held on to Bastián's hand. They smiled at each other, and he let his hand drop.

Outside, Bastián saw a fox sitting next to the well. He tipped his chin to it.

"Thank you," he told it. "He wouldn't be alive without your help."

"Nor without your blood."

From behind him, the kitsune woman stepped out from beyond a tree. She laughed at his surprised face. The fox trotted up to her and sat at her feet. She scratched it behind the ears like it was a faithful dog.

"He is well now, is he?" she asked as the fox plopped down and rolled onto its back.

"Not completely," Bastián said, "but he will be. I can see that now."

The kitsune and the fox looked at him as if he was forgetting to do something. He stood stiffly until he was won over by the fox's wagging tail. He knelt and petted its belly. Both vulpines treated him to a sharp-toothed smile.

"Hunter, another thing."

"Yes?" he asked, standing back up.

"I know he is not simply your friend. I can see the thread. Devotion such as that is unprecedented. We so often see it unrequited. Wives who have been neglected by their husbands or lustful men falling prey to a vengeful spirit. Yours is not like that. You must know you cannot marry under the laws of man. However, the spirits do not heed such laws."

"What would you suggest?"

"We have several binding rituals. Some more…intimate than others. When you are both ready, come to the temple."

"Thank you," he said.

The kitsune departed, but the fox stayed, watching him. Bastián hurried in for a small bowl of broth. He set it in front of the fox and gave it another pat as it happily lapped at it.

CHAPTER 16

Eisuke didn't look happy at his improvement. He had gained strength and weight, but he maintained a somber demeanor. Bastián knelt beside the bed and took his hand. The hand recoiled from his grasp.

"What's wrong?" he asked.

"If you're not attracted to me anymore, you can just say so."

In fairness, Bastián hadn't been very physically attracted to his withered frame before he turned. If anything, his physique had improved compared to how it was at the palace. He didn't think that type of explanation would help right now.

"Why do you think that?"

"You haven't touched me since I've woken up."

"Because you've been weak! It has nothing to do with my attraction to you."

He remained sullen, brooding with arms crossed like a petulant child. Bastián climbed onto the bed and took him in his arms. He lightly kissed his neck and shoulders. Eisuke tried to resist, but he gave in without much fight. Bastián ran a hand across his chest and another down his abdomen. He pulled him close, feeling definition to his muscles for the first time. Not even at the palace had his body felt this nice.

Bastián leaned close to his ear, his breath tickling his earlobe as he spoke. "Frankly, I think you look better like this."

Eisuke could take that as either a compliment or insult. The slight arch he felt in the oni's body as he spoke told Bastián he hadn't misjudged.

"That's a very inappropriate thing for a hunter to say."

"Is it?" Bastián said playfully. "Well, I don't think it'll compare to the inappropriate actions I'm about to take."

Bastián kissed the base of his neck, and Eisuke sharply inhaled. One of Bastián's hands crept lower down his pelvis. Eisuke reached a hand back and gripped his hip, his fingers wrapping around to caress his backside.

"Are you sure you have the strength?" Bastián asked, pausing his tease.

"I don't care if I do," Eisuke said. "I need to feel you."

"I'll go slow," he said.

Bastián undid his waistcoat and got to work on his undershirt. Eisuke stared at him with a small smirk.

"Do you hunters always have to wear so many layers?" he jested.

Bastián playfully threw his cravat at his partner's side. "Just be glad I don't wear the heavy coat around the house, too."

With the shirt undone, Eisuke reached his clawed hands up and ran them over his stomach.

"I should have let you out more," he said. "I see now palace life wasn't good for you."

Bastián smirked. "Hunting monsters, be them human or demon, is strenuous work."

"You wear it well," he said, pulling at the strings of his pants.

Bastián's smile broadened, and he kissed him, putting pressure on his chest to lay back down on the bed. Bastián guided him slowly and gently, understanding this was more for his partner's comfort than for a physical release. He paused before he got on top of him. He looked down at his partner with concerned eyes.

"I'm fine," Eisuke said. "Don't stop. Please."

Bastián did not like his shallow breath but continued lightly kissing him. He kept a hand on his chest, monitoring his palpitations as he rhythmically moved on top of him. He wanted to savor the way it felt to have him inside once again but was distracted by monitoring Eisuke's breathing. He slowed anytime it became too quick, letting himself rest atop his thighs. Eisuke let him know he was ready to continue by gripping his hips and lightly scratching the skin with his talons. He wasn't intending to mark him, but his sharp nails weren't something he could contract. Bastián let the thought of Eisuke being well enough to intentionally rake those talons across his back lead him into orgasm.

"I told you I'd top you next," he whispered when they both finished.

Eisuke laughed. It was small and weak, but it was genuine.

"Thank you," he said, "for saving me."

He wiped a strand of white hair from his face. "I had to."

Before Eisuke could say anything, Bastián hugged him tightly, pressing his face against his neck.

"I had to save you," he repeated. "Ever since I learned what happened, I searched." Tears began to form. "I searched for you even when there were no leads I could follow or trail I could track. I was desperate. If another hunter had… or if you couldn't survive the winter… you already were so badly off when I found you."

Eisuke hugged him as close as he could. His talons scratched at his back. Bastián's tears were contagious.

"I almost lost you," Bastián said. "So don't be an ass about whether I'm attracted to you or not."

Eisuke gave one strained laugh through tears. "I won't. You convinced me."

"You're weak," he said, pulling apart. He offered his arm. "Here. Take my blood."

"I don't want to hurt you," he protested.

"You won't. Well, not more than a little, anyway."

"What if I lose control as soon as I taste human blood? I don't want to endanger you like that."

Bastián chuckled. "A couple issues with that. First, you've been drinking my blood for weeks now. Second, I'm not completely human, remember?"

Eisuke looked at Bastián's arm. He felt a twinge of eerie hunger. "Are you sure I won't hurt you?"

Bastián held up his other hand. A smoky glow surrounded it. "I'm a powerful hunter, remember? I'll incapacitate you if you lose control. With love, of course."

"Okay," he said with a nod.

Bastián held his arm still as Eisuke brought his mouth to it. Eisuke first kissed it and then lightly sucked it. Then he bit down with his elongated teeth, piercing the vein. Bastián flinched at the sharp bite. It was more painful than the shallow cuts he had given himself. Yet he felt serene as he watched his partner swallow his warm blood. He had a brief worry Eisuke wouldn't be able to stop, but it felt distant from sharing his life force with him.

Eisuke let go, tenderly holding Bastián's hand. The blood pooled around the wound, but the intensity of the bleeding had significantly slowed. Bastián retracted his arm and put pressure on the puncture wound.

"Is that all you needed?" Bastián asked.

"I think so," Eisuke said, wiping at his mouth and licking any blood from his hand. "Will that stop bleeding?"

"Yeah. My veins are deep, and they clot fast."

"I noticed," he said, licking his lips.

Bastián placed some fiber at the wound site and wrapped it snugly. He then draped his arms loosely around Eisuke's neck.

"It's okay," Bastián said. "I'm here now."

"Being bloodstock to a demon is a good thing?"

"No, helping out my partner is." He pulled him in for a kiss. "Let me know if or when you feel any better."

"I already do. It's as if my head is clearer. That's the only effect so far, though."

"Good. Mine feels a bit foggier. Probably because of this." He held up his wrist. "So, I'm going to lie back down. Lie with me. Please."

There was no hesitation before Eisuke lay next to him. Bastián was relieved Eisuke's body no longer felt sickly cold. He felt a gentle scratch under his chest as the oni slowly wrapped his arms around him. Bastián shifted closer to him. He knew Eisuke wasn't very familiar with his nails yet and didn't want him to feel any guilt at hurting him, especially when it was only a scratch.

Eisuke had regained his typical build, albeit his grayish skin, white hair, red eyes, and horns remained. The pair had established a routine. Bastián fed him his blood once a week. At minimum. When feeling Eisuke's sharp teeth graze his shoulder after a deep kiss, Bastián would give him a silent nod and Eisuke would pierce the skin. Bastián felt an intense closeness when Eisuke licked up the small beads of blood. It excited him, and he encouraged Eisuke to bite and feed when relieving his own tension. Bastián wholly entrusted his body to his partner's care, and Eisuke never gave him a reason to doubt his safety.

Bastián and Eisuke traveled to the temple several weeks later. Bastián had been insistent, but Eisuke had noticeably been distressed. He didn't think a being like him belonged there anymore, but Bastián assured him it would be okay. The sight of a kitsune woman with her long tails and fox ears did not calm him.

"My lady," Bastián said, giving a bow.

"Apologies," Eisuke said, "but I am still wary of your ways."

The kitsune hid a laugh. "Do not worry, young oni. We have opinions on your kind, as well. Both as you were and as you are now."

"You told me to come to you when he was well," Bastián said.

"Ah yes," she said. "Inari has blessed you both. They would like to extend that blessing."

"Even as a hunter, they are willing?"

"They have heard your pledge. Hunt not for sport and hunt without bias, yes? If human is the cause instead of yokai, you will not show preference? Many would not pledge this, and yours has been recognized."

"What of Eisuke?" he said, looking to his partner. "He was once nobility, and I am not."

"Oh, yes, of course," she said. "Terribly sorry for your mother. I heard the hunter who killed her was not kind enough to make it quick."

"My mother?" Eisuke asked. "She died years…. I see. She wasn't my real mother."

The kitsune nodded. "Without her, the emperor likely would have let you dry to husk and keep you imprisoned until his curse was lifted. She mixed the concoction that sustained you and kept up the lie that you wouldn't survive without it."

"The tea?" Bastián asked. "I thought that was harming him."

She raised up both hands. "A little good and a little bad. She was not the kindest witch but did care that her child lived."

"The thread," Bastián said, "was that her doing, too?"

"Oh no," she said. "That is something beyond mere magic."

"Thread?" Eisuke said. He looked at Bastián. "Is it a red thread?"

"Yes," Bastián said. "When I first worshipped at one of your temples, a monk told me to watch for it. I had forgotten about it until I was searching for you, out of leads with no trace of where to go, I saw a red line in the sky. I followed it and found you."

The kitsune directed her fan toward Eisuke. "Would you like to explain, dear prince?"

"A red thread of fate," Eisuke said. "You and your destined mate are tied together with a—supposedly invisible—red thread. I can't say I fully believed in it before now."

"That is why Inari sent us kitsune to help," she explained. "The thread had gotten severely tangled but not cut. We're here to help untangle it."

"What do you propose?" Bastián asked.

"You are a very curious oni," she said to Eisuke. "A curse made in blood now drips from your thread. If you are willing to embrace that, I can bind you two together."

"I don't see how we could refuse," Eisuke said. "It is destiny."

"Mmm. Destiny in your ties, but not how difficult that journey is."

"If we agree," Bastián said, "what ritual will you perform?"

She grinned. "You are much better to speak to, little hunter, than he is. I see why my sisters have helped you before. I will forge the bond on your skin, tattooing an image of an oni as they are commonly depicted. The red ink will contain your mate's blood." She picked up a small figurine that had sat on the shrine behind her. "And I will bathe this in the blood and ink that leeches out. These will be anchors. Should you want to call the prince to your side, you manifest that with the tattoo. Should you, prince, then want to leave unseen, you may return wherever this idol is kept. Do you accept?"

"Yes," Bastián said without hesitation.

"And you?"

Eisuke looked at Bastián with surprise. "Yes, of course, I do. I didn't expect you to agree so eagerly. To bind a creature like…like me to you—"

"I know the risks," he assured him. "And I know the weight it carries. Seems silly to deny your gods, though, doesn't it?"

Bastián reached out his hand, and Eisuke took it. He squeezed it and agreed once more to the plan.

Bastián keep his client base to simple hunts around the rural area he and Eisuke had settled in. He opted for the next town over from where he had found Eisuke. He wanted to stay close to the shrine but didn't think the village would prefer his presence longer than necessary.

He knew it was temporary, but having spent nearly all the money he had on finding Eisuke, he needed to save that income before they could properly plan a permanent residence. So far from the palace and its dangers, these local villagers quickly praised the hunter's ability to resolve any of their infestations without a drop of blood to be found at completion.

As he was leaving his latest job at a bath house, the owner caught Bastián's attention.

"Please," she said, extending a note for him, "take this, too."

"Thank you," he said, holding a hand up to the offering. "That's very generous but it's not necessary."

Bastián tried to say this every time a client offered an additional gift. He had a low success rate judging by the amount of produce and home cooked meals he had back at their small house.

"Necessary?" The woman chuckled. "You have done this town a great service. I think it is necessary that a young and handsome gentleman like you spend a relaxing day here."

Bastián smiled awkwardly at her compliment. "I know this is

silly, but I don't feel comfortable in public baths."

"A private one then!" she said happily. "Tell me when you plan to arrive, and I will make sure you are given privacy."

He looked down at the note still in her hand. "Alright," he said, taking it. "Just one day."

With Eisuke's urging, Bastián found himself at the bath house not three days later. Once he was alone, he called on Eisuke with a stroke of the tattoo. They both stripped and entered the soothing waters. Between rescuing his partner and weekly hunts, Bastián hadn't taken much time to rest his body. He realized now just how much his tired muscles appreciated the heated water. They didn't do anything crude, only leaned against each other and gave a kiss or two. This was a place of business, after all.

As evening set in, they reluctantly left the warm water and toweled off. After a swift kiss, Bastián returned Eisuke to their home.

He was only half dressed when he heard footsteps behind him. Heavy footsteps. He had taken off all his weapons and talismans. Should he make a run for where they were stored? No, that was an overreaction. It had to be the evening attendant here to send him on his way.

"Finally found you," a deep voice said.

Bastián spun around and instinctively flattened himself against the wall.

"F-Frederick?" he stammered, staring at his guild mate. "How are you aliv—here? Why are you here?"

"Surprised? You led us to disaster." His hand moved to something unseen at his belt. "Been waiting to pay you back for that."

Bastián scowled, recovering his bravery. "Don't play innocent. You and the rest wanted me killed. Had I not been distracted by your failed traps, and you not distracted by a failed coup, maybe it wouldn't have happened."

"You seriously have no remorse for our fates?"

"Of course. I failed you as a leader. But what do you want me to do? Spend my days crying for a crew that betrayed me first?"

Frederick gritted his teeth. "You're right. I don't care what you think any more. You're lucky you're not my target."

"*You*," Bastián growled. "It was you who poisoned him. You're the lucky one to not have to face the guild after that."

Frederick laughed. "Please. I'd get a slap on the wrist from some and a pat on the back from others. You don't get that high up in the ranks without bending some rules."

"I won't tell you where he is."

He made a *tsk tsk* sound. "I don't need you to. I thought you were better than to let your guard down like this. Instead, you let a demon deceive you."

"That's not—" He stopped his protest. Frederick held a spiked whip in one hand. Bastián realized his plan a second too late.

The whip wrapped around his arm with trained precision. Bastián cried out in pain as the spikes cut into his skin. He saw with horror that it wrapped from his wrist to his elbow. Even if Frederick decided to simply let it go, he would still have to individually pull each studded spike from his flesh. He looked to Frederick. He could tell he had no plans of dropping the whip.

"Please," he begged in terror as he felt the leather tighten and shift. "Please, don't do this."

"You are a hunter," Frederick said, "and you have made a pact with a demon. I shouldn't even leave you with your life. Not that you deserve it."

"Don't take this out on him," Bastián begged. "He didn't—"

Frederick yanked the whip.

Bastián screamed as the flesh was torn from his arm. A mangled, glaringly red strip of shredded muscle and tendon remained. Blood cascaded from the wound and pooled on the ground. Frederick hadn't torn out an artery, but enough had been damaged to soak the ground. Bastián fell to his knees and gripped right below his elbow. His hand involuntarily twitched in anguish. He knew he had to make a tourniquet, but he could not act with such pain.

"Didn't what?" Frederick said, amused. "Capture and sentence us to death? Oh right. He did."

A shadow fell over Bastián. He managed to glance up, expecting to see Frederick. What he saw pushed the pain to the back of his mind.

Eisuke stood in front of him, guarding him. He was in his most ferocious form. His most natural form. His most inhuman form. He snarled and tensed with sharpened talons. Severing the link had unleashed him. His blood had involuntarily called him.

Frederick laughed dryly. "A blood demon, eh? That's how you were able to link it to your skin."

"Eisuke, no," Bastián begged. "Don't do this. He will kill you. Get somewhere safe."

The oni looked at his tortured partner. He couldn't leave him.

"I can't—"

Eisuke dodged out of the way just before the whip could make contact. He lunged at the hunter. Frederick blocked the attack, but Eisuke still attempted to claw his way to his throat.

Bastián didn't want to look away, but he had to try to stop his own bleeding. He tore part of his shirt and tied it above his elbow. He didn't know if he could save the arm, but he could prevent bleeding out.

Frederick threw the oni off and to the ground. With one swift move, he lassoed the demon. Eisuke shrieked as the rope tightened around him. His skin sizzled as warding magic seared him. Frederick dragged him into a sitting position and tied another length of rope around him. Eisuke screeched an inhuman sound as the ropes cut into him with every involuntary struggle.

Frederick retrieved a medium-sized glass jar and a sharp ritual knife from his pack. He carved symbols into Eisuke's chest and collected the blood that flowed from them. Frederick taunted him with the half-full bottle of his own blood.

"For you to live in," he explained to the demon's hateful sneer. He turned his attention to Bastián. "But you'll need some nourishment."

He knelt by Bastián, yanked his arm forward, and scraped up blood from the strips of flesh like he was forcing water out of a wet cloth. He let it collect into the bottle until it was two-thirds full.

"Please don't hurt him."

"It is too late for that. That thing is worse than a rabies infected feral animal."

"You don't understand. He's—"

Bastián cried out as Frederick ground his foot on his open wound.

"If you don't want it to keep suffering in those extremely painful binds, let me continue my work."

He walked back to Eisuke. He shook the bottle in front of his strained face.

"I could have let you starve," he said. "But that's your daddy's decision, not mine."

He drew his knife again and carved a different sigil into the oni's abdomen. He whispered an incantation, and the blade began to glow. He then shoved it into the middle of the sigil. The blood that poured out began wrapping his body and seeping into the cut along the knife's side. The ritual blade collected the demon's blood. Soon the body was entirely liquid. It collected in the shape of the sigil and then shot into the blade, leaving the ropes behind. Frederick emptied the blade into the bottle, now with only a few inches at the top remaining. He stored it securely at his side. He turned back to Bastián.

"I am too weak to fight you," Bastián said.

"I know. Which is why I'll leave you right where you are."

"Please, if you have any compassion—"

"Compassion for what?" He shook the jar and laughed. "This thing? Time you learn keeping a demon around as a pet has consequences."

"He's not a pet."

"I know. That has consequences, too."

"Where are you taking him?"

"You forget what our job is as hunters. The Yasunai emperor offered me a generous bounty for the capture of an oni bearing a striking resemblance to this jar of blood."

"Don't." Bastián trembled. "Don't hand him over. He'll kill him."

"Not my business. You have no idea how much money I've made on two bounties alone. You should have tried it instead of offering your body to a demon."

Bastián watched Frederick leave with his partner through heavy eyelids. He'd get Eisuke back. He had to. He repeated his determination as consciousness slipped from him.

CHAPTER 18

Bastián woke to the prodding and cleansing sting of the bath house owner dressing his wound. He was surprised he had any nerve endings left to feel the pain. The sight of his shredded lower arm reminded him of a filleted fish with the choice cuts removed.

"I'm sorry," he told the woman. "I never meant to bring violence to your business."

"Nonsense," she said. "This wouldn't be a business if you hadn't expelled the demons from it."

He stopped himself from correcting her. The little yokai had been mischievous not harmful. Demon was too harsh to call them. Trespassers, maybe, but not monsters.

Bastián stood and nearly fell. The vertigo from blood loss hit him, and he caught himself with his good hand to the wall.

"Slow down," the woman advised, taking his hand in a way both forceful and kind. "Can you make it back to your home? You must rest."

Bastián forced a smile and a nod. He'd go home, but he wouldn't rest. He couldn't without Eisuke safe by his side.

Once Bastián proved he could stand on his own, the woman went to the long burnt-out incense. She carefully picked out fresh sticks and wrapped them in bamboo paper. She handed them to Bastián.

"These will help ease the mind," she said, "so that you don't focus too much on the pain."

"My gratitude again," he said. His hand went to his pocket for the small coin bag. He gave it to her even as she tried to decline. "Please. I will not feel right if I do not offer anything for your kindness."

She accepted the payment with a soft smile. "Thank you, hunter. May you be prosperous in your work."

Bastián tipped his hat and returned home.

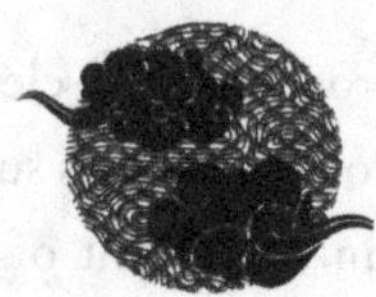

He set up a makeshift altar inside once back at his small house. He lit the incense. It smelled musky and primal, not like the floral type typically burned in the bath house. His nostrils flared as he breathed it in. He felt a frustrated rush of adrenaline as his heart raced and his muscles tightened. It was a full moon. Unlucky for him. He didn't want any distraction.

He slowly closed his fist, arm aching as the damaged tendons stretched under his shredded skin. The wound was severe even for him. He wouldn't remove the wrapping, but he knew some strips had inky black or deep red markings. The tattoo was destroyed but not obliterated.

He opened his fist and clenched his teeth as he repeated the action. A pinprick of red interrupted the white of the bandage. Good. Again. Now the blood stain was the size of a coin. He stopped straining his arm and blotted the soggy strip of bandage. Blood magic was extremely finicky. One slight misstep and the ritual did nothing. Or worse yet, harmed the conjuror. Frederick didn't take caution when he used it on Eisuke. Bastián wouldn't either.

He called to the spirits of the land. He called on the power of the moon. *Let the connection between Eisuke and me remain intact.*

Heat rushed through him, one similar to how he felt before his beast took over. He felt a need for it to break free and ravage anyone who got in his way.

Not now.

"Grant me eyes with which to see," he said to the altar. "I need to know what's happening to him."

He closed his eyes and saw red. Thick and cold blood. And tight. An uncomfortable squeeze on all parts of his body at once. Murmurs. Then words. Then—

It couldn't be.

Bastián watched the scene before him through Eisuke's red-veiled eyes. He could tell the jar was sat on a table with three men around it. He couldn't see their faces, but he knew two of the voices. The third had a cadence of imperial authority.

"Blood?" the emperor said with a laugh. "That is no proof."

"It's not just blood," Frederick said. "He's in there, trapped in spirit form."

"Ridiculous," the emperor huffed.

"Now, now," Vincente said, "that is possible. I thought you spent more of your time dozing off than paying attention to my classes, Frederick, but seems I was mistaken. If you allow me a sample of your blood, your majesty, I can prove the similarity between it and this jar's contents."

The psychic connection wavered, and Bastián lost his focus. He dropped to his knees and banged his elbows on the low surface.

"Fuck!" he cried out and clutched his wounded arm.

He scrambled up, quickly setting everything back in place on the altar. He dabbed oil, mixed it with blood, and drew a dark red X between his eyes.

"I'm not done," he growled to any spirits listening. "Bring me back there!"

The vision went red and again his muscles contracted tightly. He heard the same three voices.

"I instructed my men to send that hunter on a false lead. He shouldn't have found him."

"I do apologize, your majesty," Vincente said, *"but what does this demon have to do with my son?"*

"I hardly know or care," the emperor said. *"All I know is this thing liked to get attached to the servants. Likely tricked your son into caring about it."*

"As a servant? Not as a hunter?"

"We were ambushed," Frederick said with anger. *"Most of us were sent to be killed or sold. However, the oni took Bastián as its own."*

"You trespassed into our land without proper clearance," the emperor said calmly. *"You need to learn gratitude I thought you useful in ridding me of this nuisance."*

Bastián's vision blurred, and he dug his nails into the wood, as if trying to grasp onto this intangible bridge between him and Eisuke. A splinter stuck into the nail bed of his index finger. He didn't notice. All his attention was on maintaining the connection.

When his focus returned, he now only saw two figures at the table.

"Sloppy?" Vincente said. *"This is a rather advanced technique. Trapping a monster's spirit form. As much as I hate to admit his prowess, I will admit that."*

"Sloppy in that he left your son alive. He should have eliminated both threats."

"So, you don't believe he was tricked?"

"It doesn't matter if he was. He cared for that thing, and I do not need someone of his skills caring for a damning piece of my history."

"Let me dispose of it for you."

Bastián's conscious snapped back to the altar. "No!" His fists hit the table now covered in dark red from the blood that had dripped from his wound.

That couldn't be his father's plans. But if it weren't, he had just lied to the emperor. Bastián didn't know if his father would risk a lie to the ruler of a foreign land. He knew his father would trust him, even over the words of the emperor. But Bastián wasn't there. If Vicente thought the creature posed a risk to his son, he would eliminate it. That Bastián very much believed.

"Take me there again," Bastián pleaded. "I need to know more."

He slipped to the floor, smearing fresh blood as he went. The cloth wrapping was soaked through. Only now did he recognize how fast and shallow his breathing was. He swallowed back a dryness in his throat and felt sweat bead down his neck.

"Please," he whimpered, "One more time...." and fell unconscious.

A knock at his front door startled Bastián awake. He tried to get up, but his body screamed in pain. His back and shoulders were sore, and he didn't know how long he had been on the floor. Blood had dried making the bandage stiff and stuck to the ground. He peeled his lower right arm off the floor, the tearing sound of it grating on his ears. He cradled his arm while slowly rising to his feet.

Another knock didn't come. With a hand on his magic talisman, he approached the door. He turned the knob and quickly pushed it open, hoping to startle anyone on the other side. But there was nobody there, just a letter at his feet.

Meet with me at the tavern tonight. 8pm sharp. Don't be late.

His father's handwriting. His father who had disposed of his monstrous lover. He could hear the parental disciplinarian in those few words. His loose punctuality irritated his father and Bastián thought it rather petty to be reminded of it when Eisuke's fate was much more important.

Loaded up with the most magic defense and caution he could, and a fresh bandage, he arrived at the tavern ten minutes early. He had almost arrived thirty minutes early. Or nearly an hour, but he talked down his anxious mind. It wouldn't have made time move any faster. He scanned the crowded bar. Next, the well-lit tables near the entrance. He started towards an empty table thinking Vincente hadn't arrived yet. But then his eyes landed on a familiar face sitting in a darkened corner away from the merriment of the other patrons. Bastián froze when his eyes met his father's. He felt two very different emotions at once, and his mind couldn't decide which to enact.

He stood still in surprise until that face smiled warmly at him. Willing his limbs to move, Bastián walked towards him. He was fully aware of his breathing and fought to keep it steady the closer he got to Vincente.

"Father, I—" Overcome with emotion, Bastián hugged him. He squeezed his eyes shut, and a tear fell from them. "I'm glad you're here. It's been so bad. Everything's gone wrong."

Vincente patted him on the back as they embraced. "It's okay, son. I'll help you fix it."

"But how?" he asked, breaking apart. "Eisuke is—"

"Right here with me," he said.

Vincente pulled an unmistakable jar of blood from his pack and placed it on the table. Bastián's eyes grew wide, and he reached for it, but, shockingly, his father planted an ornate knife into the wood between him and the bottle.

"Not yet," he warned. "I haven't dispelled the enchantments yet. Frederick put extra ones on it. It'd burn your hand if you grab it."

Bastián did not attempt a reproach. Vincente poured the sake and offered some to him. Bastián declined.

"How is your arm?" he asked, gesturing to the wrapped wound.

"It is attached, and it moves," Bastián said, "so it is the best it could be."

"Frederick boasted about his attack. It doesn't surprise me he underestimated you."

"I'm more concerned with the health of my partner. Can you swear to me that Eisuke is alive?"

"As far as I can determine, yes. There is very much a living being inside here. The state he's in? That's harder to determine."

"I couldn't feel much other than a physical tightness, either, when I crossed into his mind."

"You heard us?" Vincente gave a small smile. "Of course. No wonder you look exhausted."

"Not everything," Bastián said. "But enough to know you had him."

"How many times have I warned you against using psychic techniques?" Vincente chided but without sincerity in his voice. "It will wear out your body until you cannot recover."

"As I recall," Bastián said, "you told me they were reserved for desperate situations. This very much was one."

"Indeed, it was," Vincente said, sounding proud rather than patronizing.

"I have to know," Bastián said. "Why did you send me on a mission bound to fail?"

"Oh? It failed, did it?" Vincente smugly sipped his sake. "Seems like you got something invaluable out of it."

Bastián spared him a look of annoyance. It was just like his father to try to make everything a lesson. "You couldn't have known that."

"No, but I knew what I had to do to keep you safe."

"Safe? How does any of this look like I was ever safe? Even that crew you sent me with planned to kill me."

Vincente sighed. "The guild has tired of me and the ways I've evaded their punishments. Much of that I have kept from you because I didn't want you to live in the same fear I have. Somehow, and I truly do not know how, they found out your identity. They think your masculine appearance is something I conjured so you could get preferential treatment. They feel deceived, and that, to them, is an unforgivable offense. Seeing their anger…it looked so similar to their faces the day they torched your mother's village. I had to get you out."

Bastián mimicked his father's sigh. "Why here? This wasn't safe either. You had to know the danger."

"I did, but at the time, sending you the farthest away I could think of sounded like the best thing I could do for you. I trusted either your instinct would make you decline the mission once you got here, or your experience would have you survive the danger of fulfilling it." Vincente laughed dryly. "You weren't even supposed to be with that crew. I arranged your passage and declared your position right before departure. If I had done it any sooner, the guild would have stepped in to remove you from it."

"So, I got a crew killed or enslaved I wasn't even supposed to lead."

"And then you consorted with the very devil you hunted. You don't seem torn up about their fate."

Bastián frowned. "I can't say I have much sympathy, no."

"It's fortunate our name still holds the weight your grandfather gave it. The guild, like any organization of high status, likes to cover up anything that'd negatively affect their reputation. It is why they haven't yet killed me. My personal reputation wouldn't follow you here. Only theirs. I knew you could use that to your advantage."

"And you did, too. When you met with the emperor."

He nodded. "He was willing to believe I'd punish you and dispose of his own son based on that reputation. I like to think my acting sold it, though."

"You won't be doing either of those things, will you?"

Vincente pursed his lips. "Tell me. Were you tethered to him against your will?"

Bastián shook his head. "No. I offered it first. It was more of a way for him to travel with me unseen. For his safety."

"So, he knew? About you."

He nodded, unsure which he was asking about, but the answer was the same. "He knew before I had a chance to tell him. He accepted it regardless."

"Did he know about himself?"

"No. I thought telling him about my beast form would help him with accepting his, but he took the realization hard."

Bastián fixed his eyes on the jar. He breathed in deeply, and his fingers scratched against the rough wood into a fist. Yet he didn't dare ask Vincente to release him. Vincente saw his look and took the ritual dagger from the table. He held it out to Bastián.

"Blood magic needs blood to work," Vincente said.

Bastián nodded and reached for the knife. Vincente pulled it back.

"No, no," he said. "I need your palm."

Trusting his father, Bastián gave him his hand. Vincente took it and turned it over. He carefully started carving into his son's palm. The cuts bit into his flesh deeply, deeper than Bastián was used to. Vincente looked to Bastián a few times to check if he was alright, and Bastián nodded each time, letting his father carve the key to the seal.

Once carved, Vincente turned Bastián's hand over and placed it on top of the jar. The lid sizzled under his palm. The sigil that was cut into his hand burned, growing in intensity until it felt like he had stuck his hand to hot iron. Bastián grimaced and whined, trying to keep his composure in front of his father. Bastián caught Vincente's stern stare.

"You have to withstand it," Vincente said. "The magic is trying to find a new anchor. The sigil is preventing it from going into you."

"It's…it's fine," Bastián struggled out.

Vincente's countenance briefly faltered into concern. He squeezed Bastián's wrist, and Bastián knew he was trying to comfort him. When the hissing died down, Vincente lightly lifted Bastián's hand off the lid. Molten flesh stuck to the metal and stretched like glue before he gave a swift tug that ripped the skin off.

"God damn it!" Bastián exclaimed, holding his burnt and torn hand.

"Definitely not God's magic," Vincente said. "You will be able to release him now, but I suggest waiting until you're back home."

"It better work," Bastián said. "I didn't expect to disable another body part."

Vincente sighed. "I know, but you young hunters don't understand how dangerous these magics are, to perform and to break. Consider it a last lesson."

"Last? Are you leaving?"

"I have no more business here. I need to find a place to retire. Away from you, and away from our former guild. We are safer apart, unfortunately." He held his son's unhurt hand. "I insist you accompany me to the docks. It's not safe for you to stay here any longer."

Bastián shook his head. "Not yet. I need to discuss it with Eisuke. This is his home. He needs to make the decision to leave it."

Vincente sighed sadly as if expecting this response. From his pack, he retrieved a bottle of clear liquid and a roll of bandage. He gestured for Bastián's damaged hand. He splashed the liquid onto the wound. It stung and soothed at the same time. He gently bandaged Bastián's palm.

"Be careful. Both of you," Vincente said and finished wrapping Bastián's hand. "I don't advise binding him to your blood, but if you feel you must, so be it. The longer he relies on your blood, the less susceptible he will be to other offerings."

Bastián held the jar against his chest. "We don't need alternatives. He's safe with me, and I'm safe with him."

Vincente gave him a tired nod. He dug in his pocket for a scrap of paper and handed it to him. "Here."

Bastián took the paper, reading the words written. "What is this?"

"Frederick's location. Do what you want with it. I doubt he feels any uncertainty after the wealth he just received. He's likely to stay put for a while."

"Do you think I could, I mean, should…"

Vincente smiled. "Yes, to the first. You are much more skilled than him. With a clearer mind and better focus, I doubt he could match you. As far as should, well, that's why I didn't do it myself. It's your decision."

Bastián remained silent, staring at the darkly inked words.

"I kept searching, too, you know?" Vincente said. "For any insight on controlling your beast form. Unfortunately, not much is out there on the unintended cross between curse and nature. But I recovered this." He handed him a worn journal. "My early notes from when I first met your mother. I thought it had been destroyed with the rest of the records, but I suppose I felt too sentimental. I didn't see anything obvious in there, but you may catch something I didn't. If nothing else, it's a relic of my time with her. You should have it."

Bastián gingerly accepted the journal. "Speaking of her—and all I just went through—I don't know how proud I am to be a hunter anymore."

"You fell in love with a demon," Vincente stated. "You hunted after that?"

"People and the creatures they damn need our help. Eisuke didn't choose this. Recently I've been successful at relocating the creature without harming it. I'd like to keep doing that. And there are legitimately evil spirits out there. Or evil people who control those spirits."

"Then you understand why I continue to be a hunter. It is up to you if you continue. If you don't and wish to live in peace with your mate, I would be okay with that. I think you've both earned it."

"You would?" he asked with surprise.

"Of course. You don't need my guidance any longer. While I

will always worry, I take great comfort knowing you have found someone who will love and support you." He rose and put some money on the table. "Buy him a drink for me."

Bastián looked down dejectedly. "So, this is goodbye."

Vincente patted his shoulder then drew him in for another hug. "Yes, but I know you'll be happy. I love you, my son."

Bastián hugged him tightly, closing his watery eyes. "I love you, too, father."

CHAPTER 20

As soon as Vincente had left, Bastián rushed back to his home. There, he poured out the jar's contents. At first, he thought it might have done nothing. But then the blood warbled, and Eisuke rose from the puddle. Bastián instantly embraced him despite the blood streaking his body.

"I'm so sorry," Bastián pleaded.

"It wasn't your fault," Eisuke said. "It didn't hurt in there. It was kind of like traveling through the tattoo, just more claustrophobic."

"I need to get another of those."

"Are you certain? I don't want you to ever feel you're bound to me without a choice." Eisuke held his arm and gently touched the wrapping. "Especially if someone like that hunter could so gruesomely break it."

"I don't want to hide our pact, but I think I'll go for higher up the body this time." He held up a fine bottle of sake. "Let's not think about that right now. My father said to buy you a drink, but I bought a whole bottle."

"Is this your offering to this yokai?"

Bastián nodded. "To you and to us."

"This is an exceptional quality," Eisuke said, looking at the bottle of alcohol. "Almost as good as we had at the palace."

"I thought we'd drink now and save the rest for something else worth celebrating."

"This isn't worth the whole bottle?" Eisuke said with a playful smile. He slid his hands along his waist and drew him close.

"It is, and you're overdue for a birthday present." Bastián gave him a light kiss. "We'll do what you want."

"It was probably best to have skipped it this year. It didn't end up being one of my favorites." He gently touched Bastián's cheek, sharp nails prickling his skin. "You seem like you have something on your mind."

Bastián awkwardly fumbled the paper slip out of his pocket without pushing away the arms of his partner. He held it out to him. "Frederick's location."

Eisuke looked at him with concerned understanding. "Are you sure you want to do this?"

"Don't you? He tried to kill me before you captured us, convinced your father he was worth something, killed your real mother, and nearly killed you. And also, he's an all-around mean bastard."

"I'm not against it," Eisuke said. "I did already try to have him killed once, I suppose. When I found you. I knew he seemed unsavory. I want to be certain you were okay with this. Killing someone for highly personal reasons is emotionally draining."

"You're right, but… I want my beast to do it. That's why it has to be soon. The full moon is near. Otherwise we have to wait a month, and Frederick will likely have moved on. I've dreamed about letting it go free for this exact situation. Is it okay with you that I do this?"

"Of course. And I'll gladly help. Even if just as backup."

Bastián held his necklace. "When I take this off, I need you to get it back on me after it's done. Or else I'll be unrestrained all night. Too many innocent people could get hurt."

"I'll do it. Promise."

"We need to move afterward, too," Bastián said, a rush and awkward tone in his voice. "Probably further north or to a different country."

"Why?"

"Your father wanted both me and you killed. My father lied to him and said it'd be done. We shouldn't risk staying here. Somewhere across any large body of water would be best."

"We can't go back to your land, either."

"No, not there," Bastián agreed. "But we'll find someplace. If—if you're okay to leave."

"The yokai here have been surprisingly supportive," Eisuke said, "but that's my only hesitation. If monsters across the sea have sympathy for fellow monsters, I trust we'll find a place amongst them."

"I've read of a place inhabited by creatures similar to yokai both in purpose and popularity. They're called faeries. It's a long journey, and we can take our time getting there, but I'd like to try it. Sounds like both plenty of work and plenty acceptance. Though maybe we'll find a place along the way instead. Either will be fine with me. As long as we're together."

"I'll follow wherever you lead, good hunter."

Eisuke knew he could make Bastián blush any time he called him that. The oni still knew the ways of princely flattery. Bastián used to think of his royal upbringing as a negative, but now that Eisuke had been freed from those gilded chains, Bastián liked a little indulgence now and then.

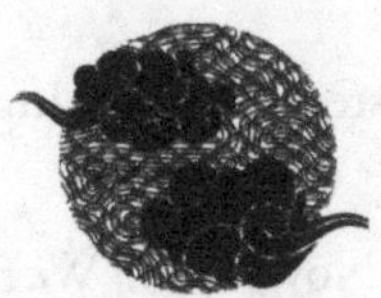

Bastián carried no weapons or magic evoking talismans. He left those at home in a place Eisuke could swiftly grab if the fight didn't go as planned. He wore only a simple robe; he didn't want to ruin any of his everyday clothes.

He had gone to the location his father gave him. Frederick was still there. Bragging everywhere he went about how skilled he was as a hunter, be it at restaurants, taverns, or brothels. He was easy to track. As arrogant as he was, Bastián knew he rarely drank enough to completely cloud his senses, even when he had no bounty to chance.

The night of the full moon came, and Bastián stealthily followed his ex-colleague until they had reached the outskirts of town. Eisuke followed, not in the tattoo, but in the shadows. Bastián had taught him some basic hunter skills as he recovered, and Eisuke adapted to his oni powers well. Still, he couldn't disguise himself as a human as other oni could, but maybe in time. For now, they had their preternatural system when they needed it.

Bastián gave a hand signal to Eisuke to halt and stay hidden. The hunter gave up his own cover and quickened his pace to be within earshot.

"Frederick!" he called.

Frederick turned around and instead of surprise, he rolled his eyes with so much exaggeration his head moved with them.

"Ugh, Bastián," he said like he had something foul in his mouth. "I knew the old man wouldn't kill you. You're looking better than I hoped though."

"Well, my arm still aches."

"That helps," Frederick said, "but I would have preferred you lost it."

"I'm not going to waste breath talking to you. You have to know why I sought you out."

Frederick laughed. "Now, now. We're both hunters here. One may be better than the other. If you want a duel, we can make it an honorable one."

"With you, I doubt it. Besides, I'm not interested in a fair fight. Just like you clearly weren't."

"Oh, what?" he said mockingly. "Do you have another demon

puppet with you?"

With a deliberate flick of the wrist from Bastián, Eisuke left the shadows and silently stepped behind Frederick, digging his talons into his shoulders. Frederick froze from the sudden piercing of his skin.

"No. The same one," Eisuke said, letting the words rasp through his sharp teeth.

Frederick gripped the handle of his spiked whip. "You bastards. Both of you. Didn't realize how true those rumors about your father were. He *is* a disgrace to the guild."

"As is his son," Bastián said. "But I've grown proud of that."

Frederick tried to yank his whip from his side, but Eisuke reacted just as fast, grabbing his arm and twisting it back.

"We met when I was still rather weak," Eisuke hissed. "If you weren't my *partner's* prey tonight, I'd feast on you myself."

Eisuke looked to Bastián, waiting for his signal. Bastián knew Eisuke was playing up his hostility, trying to get Frederick to focus on him instead. It worked, and the arrogant hunter tried to pry off Eisuke's sharp grip, squirming in his hold.

Bastián held the locket against his chest, allowing himself a moment of meditation, grounding himself to the earth. He met Eisuke's eyes and tore off the chain. Not five seconds after, he fell to the ground. His skin rippled, and a new, fur-covered spine burst from his back. His loosened robe fell from his body and onto the ground. Claws forced their way through his hands and feet. His bones cracked and his joints popped as his limbs elongated. He roared with a face not unlike a saber-toothed cat devoid of skin. His front leg was wounded and so was the pad of his left foot, but they did not affect him as much as they did in his human form.

"What the fuck!?" Frederick exclaimed, ceasing his struggle with Eisuke.

"You wanted a fight, didn't you?" Eisuke said and pushed

Frederick towards the circling feline beast. The oni deftly picked up both the pendant and robe and dashed out of the way, ready to intervene if he had to.

"Oh shit, shit," Frederick stammered. "Silver. Shit!"

Frederick frantically padded his pockets as if he had forgotten which side of his belt his gun was strapped. He tore it from its holster and fired. The bullet hit Bastián's side, and he fell back. But only briefly. Silver hurt but didn't kill. Eisuke flinched seeing it happen but knew to give his partner more time.

Bastián lunged at him, claws outstretched. Frederick dodged, deftly rolling to the side and back to his feet. He shot again but missed. Bastián caught his leg, tripping him and causing him to drop the gun. Frederick's eyes darted to the gun, but he put his hand to a serrated short sword instead. He pulled it from its sheath in time to block the claws that were coming at his face. He fought against the beast's might, and the sword's edge dug into the pad of Bastián's foot, the same one that had burned to set Eisuke free. Frederick found the strength for a sudden upward thrust, severing the connective tissue between his toes.

Bastián recoiled which allowed Frederick to get back on his feet. Bastián's front paw trailed blood as he tenderly tapped the ground with it. He shook his skeletal head and went to the edge of the circular clearing. With the gun forgotten, Frederick relied on the sword instead.

"I got you now, you fucking prick," he hissed.

Eisuke hadn't seen a true fight between hunter and beast. He himself hadn't given Frederick much of one. Bastián's injury had been too severe, and Eisuke's powers had indeed been too new to him. Watching this, anyone could see why their guild had the reputation it did. Not only would they pick a fight with a monstrous creature, but they also very well could win it. Bastián, though, was better than Frederick. As a hunter, that was. As a beast…well, that's why Eisuke was here. He'd join if Bastián needed him to.

Both beast and man had recovered their footing. Bastián jumped in the air, utilizing his hind legs over his injured front foot. Frederick dodged to the side but not far enough. The powerful landing knocked Frederick off balance, but Bastián wasn't quick enough to stop a slash from the blade cutting into his side. Fresh blood spilled onto Frederick's arm, staining his sleeve a dark wet red. Bastián turned on his haunches, landing a swift blow to the same arm that cut him. Blood of hunter and beast now mixed on both cloth and fur.

Frederick back stepped, trying to get space between them. He fumbled in his pack and Bastián knew what he was looking for. The guild had a special tonic that gave an immediate adrenaline boost so the hunter could ignore the pain. Bastián acted fast, ignoring his own pain to sprint and recover the distance between them. He lifted his uninjured forearm and slammed it down on him. He didn't have the best grip, but it was enough to finally pin him.

Bastián opened his jaws to crunch. A soft hand stopped him, gently cupping his skeletal jawbone and directing his yellow sockets to look at the oni before him.

"Hold him there a moment," Eisuke said. "You said you wanted your beast to tear apart your enemies. You can't do that with your foot like that. Allow me to be your other hand."

Eisuke touched the shredded tendons and turned into his bloody spiritual form, transporting himself into the beast's foreleg. A thick, jelly-like red substance filled the gaps in the wound as if it were a spongey fiber made solely of blood. Bastián flexed his fingers, and they moved well.

Without further hesitation, Bastián sunk his massive claws deep into Frederick's chest. Each clawed finger sliced between a rib bone, piercing his lungs. Frederick could no longer scream, but he could still feel. Bastián pulled his arms apart, opening the ribcage like a stubborn double door. The sternum was tough, and Bastián looped his jaws around it, crunching down and breaking it. Cartilage and muscle stretched and popped as Bastián continued to pull until the bones on either side snapped under the pressure. With the chest cavity fully exposed and the faintly beating heart in view, Bastián paused before taking the organ between his jaws and squishing it across his teeth. He reared his head back, tearing the heart from the chest and then spitting it back out into the cavity as if second-guessing its tastiness.

Eisuke raced out of Bastián's body. He held his head delicately in his hands as he had done before.

"It's over," Eisuke said. "Come back to me."

Bastián's form stood motionless. Eisuke leaned in and licked the blood from his oversized, exposed canine tooth. The beast shook and whined. He stepped back from the oni, clawed hands over his skull. With sickening pops and cracks, the form folded in on itself, and Bastián returned to his human appearance.

He stared at Eisuke, bewildered. Then at the moon. It was still full. He took a stride towards him, but fell to one knee, gripping an arm that trembled and tensed as claws grew from it.

Eisuke rushed to him and pushed the locket to his chest. Instantly, the transformation stopped. Bastián panted and put his own hand over Eisuke's. The oni handed him the robe as well and Bastián put both on, albeit immediately staining it with his blood-covered body.

"Thank you," Bastián said. "I almost lost myself again."

"You came back though. Briefly."

"I never stopped a transformation before. That means it's possible!"

Bastián hugged him. Eisuke hugged him back but then took his hand in his, examining the wounded fingers.

"Will you be okay?" he asked, looking worriedly at the deep

cuts. "You were already injured enough before this fight."

Bastián nodded. "I wasn't using it much anyway. Just added a few more days to its recovery." He twisted his torso and grimaced. "How comfortable are you with digging out a bullet?"

Eisuke flexed his own talons. "Do you think these would make that easier or harder?"

"Maybe we should ask the kitsune. If we haven't run out of blessings from them yet."

"I'll be sure we give them a generous offering." He stroked the top of his head and then kissed it. "Let's get you home. As I recall, we have an exquisite sake waiting for us there." Eisuke pressed his forehead against his. "I love you, good hunter."

"I love you, too, my beautiful monster."

"I know we need to go somewhere new, but can I have one request?"

"Anything."

"We stay another month. That's when the sakura bloom, and you really must see it."

"Of course," Bastián said. "We need to prepare for a long voyage after all. There's no need to rush as long as we don't do anything too noticeable."

"Oh, we probably need money then. But it's too risky to do hunts."

Bastián's eyes landed on the distorted form at his feet. He knelt and examined the pockets of his coat. He heard a jingle of coins and retrieved a bag from one of the inner pockets.

"No one will think too hard about a hunter being killed by his prey," Bastián said, holding the coin purse up. "And this whole town knew he had money. Someone else will take it if we don't."

"Usually I'd frown at that," Eisuke said, "but it is money from my father given for my blood. Besides, it'd still go to the hunter who captured me."

Bastián was momentarily confused then rolled his eyes. "Don't say anything corny."

Eisuke grinned and kissed him. They returned home and drank to their nightmare ending and their dreams beginning.

I want to thank Andrew Forrest Baker who has been an amazing editor and cheerleader throughout the publishing process. I also want to thank everyone at Parlyaree for their work and belief in my writing. Publishing your first novel is scary; their advice and excitement helped make it less so. To Di Quartel who first introduced us and always tries to make long tattoo sessions as painless as possible, you have my thanks.

A heartfelt thank you to Laura and Ellen who are always an ear for when science doesn't go the way we want it to. As well to Ty and Maddie for listening to the paragraphs of text I send you even if we can't be in person. And of course, to my sister Amy who may not love my writing style but still supports me.

Last, a very good chin scratch to my cats who sit with me when I'm writing and sometimes it's not just because they want food.

Founded in Atlanta, Georgia in 2023, PARLYAREE PRESS is dedicated to publishing writing that expands, reveals, and interrogates the mainstream. We seek out fiction, creative nonfiction, and poetry that exists in the liminal space between what was and what will be.

The cant of circus performers, freaks, queers, and thespians, Parlyaree is the invented language required to tell the stories of those othered, to keep their secrets, to keep them safe. It is a polyglot of experiences that may only be told in one's own voice. Parlyaree—as an invented language—borrows from what was to create something new.

That is what excites us at Parlyaree Press. Stories that transform; essays that reimagine; poetry that takes us behind the stanza to the core of our being and back again; language that plays as much as it conveys.

Writers: tell us your secrets.
Readers: reimagine your worlds.